Dental Sting

- a murder mystery set in Glasgow

M. MacGregor

Published in 2018 by
Moira Brown
Broughty Ferry
Dundee. DD5 2HZ
www.publishkindlebooks4u.co.uk

ISBN13: 978 1 97337 260 8

Front cover:
Entrance to Rogano restaurant, 11 Exchange Pl, Glasgow.

About the author

The author was brought up in Fife, Scotland. She studied Architecture in Glasgow, Dundee and Newcastle. She lives in the picturesque seaside town of Broughty Ferry but misses the vibrance of Glasgow. This is her second murder mystery novella.

Acknowledgements

She gratefully acknowledges the help given by her husband Eric, her brother-in-law Christopher, and her nonagenarian father Ian who painstakingly proofread the manuscript.

Disclaimer

PART ONE
FILLING UP TO MURDER

His white teeth glisten like the powdered snow beneath his feet. He pulls his goggles down over his healthy blue eyes and pushes away from the mountain top.

He carves down the mountain, moving from side to side, drinking up the scenery as he goes. This is his last descent before hitting the bars in Verbier with his young fiancé. Tomorrow he'll return to Scotland where the drilling, filling and pulling will begin again in earnest to keep him in the lifestyle to which he has become accustomed.

"2nd upper right…"

"Ouch!"

"…is crumbly."

"A O (I know)."

"There's not much left of it, I'm afraid, Mr Evans."

Putting down his tool, respected dentist Simon Balding peels off gloves as his patient rinses his mouth.

"Do you think you can save it, Mr Balding?"

"I'm afraid that won't be possible. The tooth is rotten."

"There it is again," interrupts the dental assistant.

"There's what again?"

"The bleeping."

"Did you hear anything Mr Evans?"

His patient responds after spitting in the bowl. "My hearing's no' great."

"My hearing is fine and I didn't hear anything. Rachel reckons there's some bleeping sound coming from the attic."

A faint chirping noise sounds again.

"Did you hear it that time?" Simon's assistant asks, losing patience.

"Yes I did, Rachel. I heard it that time, but if you don't mind, Mr Evans and I have more serious things to discuss."

The dentist's patient swings his legs round and perches on the edge of the examination chair. He looks directly into his dentist's eyes pleading for an inexpensive solution. "What are my options, Mr Balding?"

"There's no point in discussing options at this stage, Mr Evans. We can run through those after the extraction..."

"Extraction!"

"Afraid so. And the sooner the better." Simon Balding takes a deep breath before raising his voice. "We don't want any disease to enter your gums."

"Gum disease?"

Simon Balding adds, "That would be my concern if we do nothing."

To signal the consultation has come to an end the dentist removes his patient's coat from a peg on the back of the surgery door. "You'd better arrange an appointment on your way out."

Simon Balding's next patient shuffles into the consultancy chair.

"And how is the family, Mrs Grant?"

"Very well, thank you."

"Oh good."

"That's our youngest just left for Edinburgh University so the house is very quiet."

"Oh, excellent. What is she studying?"

She replies, "History and Spanish," as she lowers her head on to the reclining chair.

"I'm sure she'll have the time of her life. Now, have you been having any problems with your teeth since you last visited?"

"No, none at all. I'm just here for a checkup."

Simon places a blue plastic cover over his mouth and ties the elastic bands around his ears. "Okay dokey. Are you ready Rachel?"

"Yes, Mr Balding."

"Okay, open wide, please?"

Mrs Grant opens her mouth then closes her eyes and tries to remember whether or not she turned off the oven before leaving the house. The words and numbers about to be read out by her dentist to his assistant mean nothing to her, but she trusts Simon Balding to look after her teeth, just as she trusted his father before him.

"… Lower right 25, lower left 24… Lower right 28, overlap lower right 27."

Simon Balding pauses. "Have you thought about doing anything about these squint teeth, Mrs Grant?" He removes his hands from his patient's mouth to allow her to answer.

She laughs, "What at my age? I'm no spring chicken."

"What do you mean, at your age?" He smiles causing little crows feet to appear at the outer edges of his eyes. "These days it's not just the preserve of youngsters to have their teeth straightened."

"Seems a bit vain to me."

"Not at all, Mrs Grant. I have a client aged 72 who has just had a brace fitted."

"Really!"

Simon realises he is half-way to talking his client round. He knows she can afford it and he guesses, judging by her designer spectacles, she may well err on the side of vanity. "And, if you pay a bit extra you can have clear braces fitted so no one would even notice."

Cheerily she replies, "It would be nice to be able to smile with confidence. I'll have to consult my husband though."

Simon Balding relaxes, safe in the knowledge her husband is a pushover, having recently sold him a gold filling. "Of course. We have an offer on clear braces that lasts until the end of the month."

"If it makes me look better I'm sure he wouldn't mind." Mrs Grant is confident that she wears the trousers in her household. "How much would it cost roughly?"

"My receptionist can take you through our dental plans on your way out."

Simon signals to his patient she is required to open her mouth again.

"Lower left 29..."

Bleep.

"There's that bleep again."

Mrs Grant pulls away to speak, "A battery in a smoke alarm might be running out."

His assistant is exasperated, "Honestly Simon it's really doing my head in."

"I don't know what it can be. All our smoke alarms run off the mains." He motions for Mrs Grant to lean back and continues where he left off.

Nigel Wang, dentist number two, knocks gently and pops his head round Simon's door.

"Are you busy?"

Simon pulls off his gloves to signal he is finished. "I think we're done here." He smiles charmingly at his well-heeled client. "Mrs Grant here looks after her teeth, flosses every day, unlike most of our patients."

"Simon, would you please investigate where that annoying noise is coming from?"

"Okay, okay Nigel." He looks at Mrs Grant, "Nigel has an especially sensitive ear. He trained as a concert pianist you know."

Mrs Grant's mouth falls open as she forgets all about her squint teeth. "Really? So why aren't you doing that now?"

Nigel replies flatly, sadly even, "It was not easy to pay bills."

"I'll get a ladder and take a look. Rachel's pretty certain the sound's coming from the attic."

"May be a battery running out of juice."

"That's what I said," Mrs Grant adds, smugly.

"I've no idea what it could be Nigel. As I've already mentioned to Mrs Grant, since the building was refurbished all our smoke alarms run off the mains so there's no need to worry. We'll be well warned if there's a fire."

Simon Balding climbs the first few rungs of an aluminium stepladder and flips open the hatch. His colleague holds the ladder steady as he climbs to the top of the steps, onto the platform and into the attic.

"As far as I know there's nothing up here…" Simon's voice becomes fainter. "…apart from some boxes belonging to my dad."

His colleague pops his head through the hole in the attic floor. "Sounds interesting."

"Not really, it's just old photographs from his time in India." Nigel hears Simon stumbling. "I wish I could find the light switch."

Bleep.

"The sound is coming from the left hand side." Nigel can barely make anything out. "Try the eaves."

Simon fumbles about in the dark. "It's a small space. The eaves are blocked off. There's a little door somewhere."

"Simon, wait, I'll go get a torch."

"I've found a latch."

Bleep.

Nigel Wang hears the sound of a metal latch being lifted, then a door scraping open as Simon crawls inside.

"Buzzzzz!"

Then a piercing scream. "Ahhhhhhhhhhhh!"

"Buzzz! Buzzz! Buzzz!"

Louder bleep.

A swarm of wasps flies by Nigel's shocked face, before escaping down through the hole in the attic floor.

"Help me!"

"Buzzz! Buzzz! Buzzz!"

"Simon, are you alright?"

"Ahhhh!"

"Buzzz! Buzzz! Buzzz!"

His colleague, doing his best to dodge the constant stream of wasps, climbs into the attic."

Bleep.

"Simon!!!!"

"Ahhhh!"

"Buzzz! Buzzz! Buzzz!"

Nigel Wang's eyes gradually become accustomed to the dark. He crawls in the direction of the wailing and can now make out his colleague writhing on the floor, grasping his face in his hands, clearly in agony. Now, afraid to open his own mouth for fear of wasps entering, all Nigel can do is blink, to convince himself this is really happening. He kneels beside the fallen body, flapping his hands to try to prevent more wasps landing on Simon's face. His efforts are fruitless. He is powerless to save his colleague whose cries soften as his movements lessen. His kicking eventually stops.

Groping the timber roof trusses Nigel's hand finally rests on a light switch. He flicks it to on, thus illuminating the ghastly scene.

Flinching, Nigel's eyes narrow to lessen the horror of what he sees before him; his 'born with a silver spoon in his mouth' boss lies on the floor, his mouth gaping open, his face frozen. A solitary wasp crawls inside. As he shakes the lifeless body he whispers, "Simon!!!"

No answer.

Simon's face is bloated and covered in lesions. Nigel Wang feels for a pulse. There is none.

PART TWO
THE INVESTIGATION

Lorna is not pleased at having to put down the piece of charcoal and make excuses to leave her life-drawing class at the Glasgow School of Art.

As she walks backwards towards the door she waves apologetically at the brave, naked model who can only use his elderly eyes to acknowledge her. He responds with a wink. She laments the fact that whenever she tries to pursue a hobby someone, somewhere, spoils it for her by dying.

*

Lorna slowly opens the dental surgery door.

"Buzzzz." Several wasps escape.

A Scene of Crime Officer hands her a plastic suit.

"The body's in the attic, Ma'am. Not a pretty sight."

"Thanks."

"You can gain access from the 1st floor landing."

As Lorna climbs the staircase, she passes a series of backlit, box-framed photographs showing smiling good-looking people of various ages with terrific teeth.

On the landing a police officer holds a ladder steady to allow the police doctor to descend. Reaching the bottom, he brushes a wasp from his arm, and removes a mask and plastic hood revealing reddish hair with a neat matching beard and full moustache. His face seems familiar, but Lorna cannot think where she has met him before.

Lorna holds out her hand. "I'm Detective Inspector Gunn."

He removes a plastic glove. "Dr Hughes. Delighted to meet you. Gunn, now that's a good Highland name. I've relatives in the Caithness area." He proceeds to step out of the SOCO suit to reveal a dapper tweed jacket and matching waistcoat.

"My husband's from Thurso, I'm from Greenock myself."

"Ah, Thurso." A gentle smile and gaze suggest the mere mention of the name has brought back happy memories. "I had to leave a dinner party you know. And the food was first class." He takes a comb from his pocket and combs his short, thick hair.

"Dr Hughes, are you able to determine the cause of death?"

He straightens his clothing, "Anaphylaxis."

"Which is?"

"A severe allergic reaction to stings. In this case wasp stings."

"Really?"

"The wasps plant venom, Inspector. Some people's immune system simply can't handle it. The body shuts down, each sting making matters worse. Simon Balding disturbed an active wasps' nest. And they went for him good and proper. Vicious little creatures."

"You're telling me."

"I've arranged for the body to be moved to the mortuary; once you've seen it of course and the SOCO officers are satisfied they've collected all their data."

"Thank you, Doctor."

"I wouldn't venture up there if you're at all allergic to wasps."

"Don't worry, I'm not." Lorna can think of several occasions in her life when she'd been stung and had no adverse reaction.

"You Grenockians are made of stern stuff."

She smiles and nods. "Are you absolutely sure Doctor, that no foul play is involved?"

"Yes, certain. There are no pressure marks on the dentist's throat or anywhere else on his body. So, there is nothing to suggest another person was involved."

"Thank you, Doctor."

DI Gunn turns to the uniformed police officer, "Have Simon Balding's relatives been informed yet?"

"Yes. The deceased's family live in the West End of Glasgow. Officers are on their way now to inform his mother and..." He refers to a notebook "sister. His fiancé is flying up from London."

"Tragic."

"Sure is, Ma'am."

"His colleague, the dentist who found him, is waiting in the consulting room if you want to speak to him." Flipping over a few pages in his notebook he adds, "His name is Dr Nigel Wang. Originally from Hong Kong."

"Is that relevant?"

"No, Ma'am. Not that I know."

"Have you taken a statement yet?"

"Yes, Ma-am."

"Good, then tell Dr Wang he's free to go."

Lorna climbs the ladder, fully kitted out in the plastic SOCO uniform to avoid contaminating any evidence. She disappears into the foosty-smelling attic.

The forensic photographer carefully crawls out from within the eaves, through the small doorway clutching a digital SLR camera hooked up to a flash unit.

"Is that you done?" Lorna enquires as the man edges towards the hole in the floor.

"Just about. I'm going out for a smoke."

Lorna peers into the eaves. A dim electric light bulb illuminates a SOCO officer who is carefully dusting a smoke alarm with aluminium powder in order to eke out fingerprints. If found, she'll preserve each one by making a print with clear tape and sticking it to card. Lorna knows better than to interrupt this important, painstaking work by blethering.

The SOCOs have told her the wasps' nest is located at the furthest, narrowest point, but she can't really make it out due to its camouflaged nature. The only evidence proving these stripy, noisy, vicious little insects are the killers is the unsightly, lifeless body with wasp bitten face lying before her. A wasp crawls out from inside an ear across the spotty, swollen face frozen in time.

It suddenly dawns on Lorna who the doctor downstairs reminds her of; he looks just like Vincent Van Gogh in a self-portrait hanging in the Musée d'Orsay she saw on a visit to Paris. The portrait was painted at a time when both his ears were intact. Lorna is glad she didn't embarrass herself by saying, "Don't I know you from somewhere?"

"Who is in charge here?"

A slim, tall woman with long flowing hair has just burst into the surgery. "I'm Simon Balding's fiancé." She flashes a large, diamond engagement ring in the faces of the police officers as proof.

Lorna, having returned to the safety of the ground floor, steps forward, "I am. Detective Inspector Gunn. And you are?"

"Bryony Jenkins. Simon's fiancé." She waves away a wasp. "Can I have a word please?... In private."

"It's only police here Miss Jenkins."

"Well, in that case, I'll tell you *all* what I think."

"And what is that exactly?" DI Gunn is all ears.

Her heavily made up eyes narrow. "I don't, for a minute, believe this was an accident."

Lorna is taken aback. "You don't? And why's that?"

"Because… it is all a bit too…" She takes a deep breath, before adding, "…well timed."

*

Lorna slumps into a worn brown-leather armchair and swings her feet up onto its matching stool.

"Here!" Colin places a book in her lap. "I thought you might enjoy it."

She picks it up. *The Naked Civil Servant.* What is it?"

"It's Quentin Crisp's outrageous autobiography.'

"Why do you think I'll like it? Wasn't he flamboyantly gay?"

"Because…" Colin flops onto the sofa. "it's quite funny… and tragic in equal measure and… he was a 'naked civil servant'. An artist's model. He posed naked at art schools as a means of income. He was always poor, up until the age of about 70 when that book you're holding was made into a film starring John Hurt. So, how was your first life drawing experience? Was it a man or a woman?"

"A man. I ended up with the worst view because I was late."

"What was so bad about it?"

"Colin! use your imagination."

"I'm trying to, but I can't imagine a good view."

"Now I know how ghastly and wrinkled you're going to look in twenty years time."

"Oh, thanks, and here was me making you a lovely supper." On hearing the sound of toast popping up, he picks himself up from the sofa. "Want butter on your toast or would you prefer toasted cheese? That'll take longer."

"Buttered toast is fine."

He walks through to the adjoining room.

Lorna raises her voice, "I had to leave the class early because I got a call out."

"Oh no!" he calls back.

"A 28 year old dentist was killed…"

"Oh dear."

"You'll never guess by what?"

"A horse?"

"Close – a wasp – or several of them."

Colin laughs instinctively because it sounds so implausible. He re-enters the room carrying a tray.

Lorna continues, "A horrible accident we think, but there may be more to it. Doubt it though. How was the library today? Any strike action in the offing?"

"No, but that wily old dear Agnes Connelly chained herself to the library railings this afternoon. She and the 'friends of the library' are protesting against the closures. She had arranged for a local newspaper to cover the story. She's something else that woman."

"Old people are so…"

"Militant?"

"Yes, militant compared to the young. Take Daisy. She's so little interest in politics it's embarrassing."

"That'll surely change. She called by the way. Asking if we fancy visiting Dundee next weekend. She appears to have a new boyfriend. He's on the same course."

"Yes, that would be nice. I could do with a break."

"I thought we could treat ourselves and stay one night in the new Malmaision hotel. Well, it's old but new inside."

"Sounds brilliant, Colin. Please book it immediately. Jenny's off to Athens. Jamal, India. Alistair, Turkey (to play golf of course) and I'll be able to boast I'm going on a mini-break to Dundee. This new case will be wrapped up soon enough. I'm certain the guy's fiancé is wrong. That it wasn't deliberate." She takes a sip of tea, "How could it be?"

*

Lorna leans against a desk holding a disposable cup of coffee in one hand and a marker pen in the other.

"The cause of death was Anaphylaxis."

"Which is?" Alistair sits casually swivelling in a black-leather chair.

"A severe allergic reaction." She takes a sip of coffee. "There had been a bleep coming from the attic for a while and Simon Balding went up to investigate. When he crawled inside the eaves he disturbed a live wasps' nest. That's when the poisonous little beasts unleashed hell on him."

Jenny is squeamish. "Yuck!"

"Yuck indeed, Jenny. His face was stung several times and was horribly red and swollen. He was dead within minutes of the first sting."

Techie Jamal asks the most obvious question. "What's there to investigate, Boss?"

"The pushy fiancé's rich, pushy father has already been on the phone to the Super threatening to report us to the complaints commission if we don't carry out a thorough investigation."

"Alistair, what did Mandarin say to that?"

"Chief Inspector Russell said he's off to Majorca tomorrow for a fortnight and assured the chap he's assigned a family liaison officer and put his very best team on the case."

"Was he talking about us?" asks Detective Sergeant Jenny Brown who was brought up on the Isle of Lewis amongst people not prone to boasting. She also has a Law degree from Glasgow University and likes to talk.

"Of course he was meaning us, Jenny. He did say, though, he wants the case wrapped up before he returns."

Chief Inspector Darren Russell has recently bought a nice little apartment in the Port de Pollença with the intention of spending more time there on his retirement from the police after, according to DI Gunn, '30 years of mediocre service'.

Lorna adds, "He's planning to write comedy sketches to send in to the BBC."

Alistair chips in, "I've got one. What about a character, maybe a Chief Inspector, who makes his team investigate a guy who gets killed by a wasp? They tell him to buzz off."

"That's more like a joke you'd find in a Christmas cracker." Jenny adds, "A really cheap one."

DI Gunn grins. She loves the fact her small team gets on so well. Dealing with death on a day-to-day basis is depressing enough without having to work alongside a partner whom she would willingly strangle, which has been the case in the past. She is grateful now that the people she spends more time with than even her husband Colin are so decent. "Alistair, you wouldn't be laughing if it was your relative who'd been killed by a wasp."

"Oh, I don't know, Boss. I have way too many relatives. I can only inherit a pittance, if that."

Lorna coughs. "The grief-stricken fiancé, we don't yet know if she's mentioned in the will, is shored up in Babbity Bowsters. Alistair and I will go there this afternoon to interview her. We'll head off once I hear back from forensics."

"You." Lorna points at Jenny then Jamal. "Find out everything you can about Simon Balding - his financial situation, his relationships, his family.

Find out when the dental surgery was refurbished. The names of tradesmen. Leave no stone unturned."

*

As Lorna rests her back against the grey painted wood panelling, she marvels at the interior of this bar which has changed so little in thirty years. Oscar Marzaroli's stylish black and white photographs still adorn the walls showing characterful faces of street traders of yesteryear.

Alistair places two coffee cups on the table.

"They've phoned up to her room. Told her we're here."

The clicking sound of high heeled shoes precedes the immaculate vision that is Bryony Jenkins.

"Hello," she says in a more subdued fashion than during DI Gunn's first encounter the previous evening.

They both stand up.

"Miss Jenkins, this is Detective Constable Boyle."

She stretches out a thin arm in the direction of Alistair. She is wearing an expensive-looking starched white blouse.

"Pleased to meet you Miss Jenkins. I'm really sorry about your loss."

"Thank you." Bryony uses her hand to wipe away a tear from her cheek. They sit down and the two detectives wait until she regains her composure.

Alistair flips open his black notebook. "Where did you meet your fiancé, Miss Jenkins? When you met him for the first time, I mean."

"At a party. It was in a flat in the Docklands area of London. One of my friends was having a leaving party. Fenella was taking a break from art school to travel round India. Simon was at the party."

"Where was he living at the time?"

"In Glasgow. He was down visiting friends. They'd all gone to Newcastle Uni together. That's where Simon studied dentistry."

"Are you still at art school?" asks Lorna. "It's just you don't look like many art students we have around here."

"I'm in my final year studying fashion at Chelsea College of Arts."

Alistair is determined not to miss his game of golf tonight. "Did none of Simon's friends or relatives invite you to stay with them last night?"

"It was a whirlwind romance. I've only visited Glasgow once before to meet Simon's family. It's a lot nicer than I thought it would be."

"Glad you like it," Alistair responds a bit too sarcastically. Alistair has never been to Chelsea, but he once heard a guy in the Met say the Scottish accents in that area usually belonged to homeless people.

Bryony pushes her smooth, shiny long blonde hair behind her ears.

"Simon and I tended to meet in more stylish European cities – like Paris or Milan."

Lorna interjects, "More stylish than Glasgow?"

"Just a bit." She gently giggles. "Or we went skiing, usually to Verbier where he owned a chalet."

Holding his mobile phone underneath the table Alistair glances at a new text message 'Tee booked 5:54pm'. He replies with a thumbs up emoji.

"How did you get on with Simon's mother here in Glasgow?" asks Lorna already suspecting she didn't.

"I didn't take to any of them to be honest. I could tell instantly they didn't like me. You should have seen his mother's face when I told them my father is a merchant banker."

"Did that not go down well?"

"Down well? And his dowdy sister showed hate in her eyes when I said he had stood as a candidate for the Conservative Party. Are all Scots jealous of success Inspector Gunn?"

"Eh, possibly."

"Supposedly his father was a more reasonable human being, but I never met him. He died before I met Simon. Simon took over his dental practice, but I suppose you already know that. That's why he returned from London.

"Did he do that to please his father, d'you think?"

"Partly. Also, the surgery had just been renovated. His father had invested in a lot of new equipment, but it was Simon who transformed it into a really profitable business."

"His father wasn't expecting to die then." Alistair calculates he couldn't have been that old.

"No. Cancer. He was dead within six months of the diagnosis."

Alistair shudders. "Terrible."

"Simon told me his sister turned on him at the time, when their father was dying, because, according to her, he wasn't visiting often enough. But how could he if he lived in London?"

"It couldn't have been easy for them. Miss Jenkins, did you know Simon was allergic to wasps?"

"No."

"He never mentioned it?"

"No, but I'm damn certain his family knew."

Lorna replies, "That has still to be determined. We don't yet know if he knew himself." She glances at her watch. In twenty minutes time Colin will be standing waiting for her outside a restaurant in Mount Florida. She promised she wouldn't be late. "Miss Jenkins, what makes you suspect Simon's death was not purely an accident?"

Bryony opens her handbag and withdraws a white envelope. She places it on the table.

"I have proof, Inspector…" She pushes the envelope towards DI Gunn. "… that Mrs Balding did not want me to marry her son."

Lorna removes two sheets of paper from the envelope addressed to Bryony Jenkins, Beaufort Street, Chelsea, London.

"I've underlined in pencil the relevant bits."

Lorna scan reads the letter, focusing on the highlighted sections,

Bryony, I beg you to wait a while, please wait until you know each other better. Marriage is such a big step. ...

I don't believe Simon has recovered from his last serious relationship. I know when Kirstin ended their engagement he was devastated. ...

The last words before Anne Balding's signature are *Marry in haste, Repent at leisure.*

"I can see this is an unfortunate turn of events for you Miss Jen…"

"Unfortunate, Inspector? Unfortunate?"

Lorna searches for a better word. "Tragic?"

"It's horrific. I was due to be married in three month's time." She rubs her eyes and sniffs. "Now, the life I imagined is gone." She closes her eyes and swallows. "Gone."

DI Gunn drains the last drop of coffee from her cup. "Miss Jenkins. Bryony. I realise you're upset, and I don't doubt his mother was none too keen, but this letter doesn't prove anything other than she thought you were being too quick in marrying her son."

"It is a motive, Inspector. Don't you understand? She and the sister inherit the lot. Isn't money usually the motive behind murder?"

"She's a good-looking girl, Bryony."

"I knew you'd say that," Lorna responds. "Rich people have a habit of looking better than their poorer counterparts."

"True." Alistair presses his foot on the brake as the traffic lights change from amber to red.

"I suspect she's talking a lot of rubbish about Simon's family. It's all supposition. She hardly knew them. Only met them once. I'm on the mother's side. What was the big rush? Was she frightened he might change his mind?"

"The pushy fiancé's father seems to have a lot of clout."

"Must have friends in high places."

Alistair glances upwards. The light remains red. "Crazy. It's not like anything we do is gonna bring the poor guy back."

"Bryony's father must be heart-broken his credit card isn't going to get a rest any time soon."

Horns sound and fumes fill the air causing Alistair to press the electric button to close the tinted windows of the Passat. He glances up at the Tolbooth clock. The light finally switches to green.

"If I put my foot down now we'll both make it on time." The car speeds off.

"Put it in cruise control, Alistair. Set it to 30. I'd rather be late than sorry."

*

Lorna waters her money plant and returns to reading over the witness reports. She has put in a request to see the deceased's medical records and is waiting for someone from the Fire Brigade to call.

Technie Jamal passes the open door and gives it a knock.

"Got a minute, Boss?"

"Yeh, sure, Jamal. It's not like you to communicate with me in person. Great stuff. You'll find it's a lot quicker than sending emails to and fro. Take a seat."

"Yeh, I know, I'm trying to change." He sits down in the chair opposite.

"Is it true you have a girlfriend, Jamal?"

"Eh, yeh. Who told you?"

She taps her nose, "I have my sources. Where'd you meet her then?"

"Online."

She laughs. "So, what have you got for me?"

"I searched the web and found a spreadsheet listing payouts made to NHS dentists. Out of nearly three thousand NHS dentists in Scotland, last year, Simon Balding was in the top fifty highest earners; and that wouldn't include the work he did privately

– implants and other procedures not available on the NHS."

"Interesting."

"Three people have threatened to sue him since he took over the practice."

"Well done. We now have three people with a motive."

Lorna's phone rings. "Excuse me, this'll be the Fire Brigade."

Jamal rises and mouths, silently "Okay" and leaves the room as Lorna lifts the receiver.

"DI Gunn... Oh, Mr Jones. Thanks for calling back... Oh you were were you? Congratulations. I've never been much good at table tennis myself."

*

"What d'you think about this case, Jamal?"
"A waste of time."

"Why?" Jenny flips through pages of printouts that Jamal has gathered on Simon Balding's financial situation.

"Cause it isn't possible to plant a live wasps' nest in the eaves of an attic."

"Yeh, you're right, but it is possible someone planted a smoke alarm up there next to it."

"What, and wait a few years for it to bleep?"
"It's possible."

"Possible, but not likely." Jamal is fed up of Jenny's conspiracy theories. She even suspects 9/11 may have been an inside job.

When he hears Lorna's footsteps coming along the corridor, Alistair hits the pause button on a golf instruction video playing on his phone. He is determined to cut out this slicing problem that has recently entered his game; occasionally curving the ball right off the tee is wrecking every round. Alistair desperately hopes he can improve before he plays the next round of the Club Championship.

Lorna walks to the front of the room, stands by her white board, picks up a marker pen and reads out as she writes, "What we know so far."

"Simon Balding died from multiple wasp stings." Using a magnet, she pins a photo of Simon Balding's bloated, bitten, badly-swollen face to the board. "According to his last two patients, the dental assistant kept complaining about a bleeping sound, urging him to find out where it was coming from. His last patient said Dr Wang came at the end of her consultation and also complained about the noise. We know he held the step ladder to help Simon Balding climb into the attic. Those two people lured him up there so we need to find out more about this colleague, Dr Nigel Wang, and the dental assistant Rachel Devine. Jenny and Jamal, you find out if they bear any grudges. If they have a motive to harm him."

Lorna places a photo of the smoke alarm on the board.

"The smoke alarm is approximately five years old, but, according to a fire officer, the battery inside is older."

"Is that significant?"

"Could be, Jenny. The manufacturer stopped making this battery before that type of smoke alarm came into circulation. And he doubts very much that Simon Balding Senior would have put an old smoke alarm battery lying around the house into a new smoke alarm.

Jenny admits, "It's the sort of thing I'd do." Her eyes light up. "Maybe he added an old battery deliberately so it would go off quicker. Maybe," Jenny's imagination is going into overdrive, "…he planted the smoke alarm up in the attic, next to the wasps' nest, for his son to find?"

Alistair is skeptical. "So, you're saying Simon Balding may have been murdered by Simon Balding Senior deceased?"

"Alistair, think about it, it's the perfect murder. Bumping someone off *after* you've gone. You can't be sent to prison if you're already in a coffin."

"His fiancé did say he hardly visited his father after the cancer diagnosis." Alistair shakes his head, "What am I saying? It's crazy."

Jenny's on a roll. "Maybe Simon Balding broke his father's heart. Children can do that. My mum's uncle spoilt his daughter rotten and when she was twenty-two she left for Australia, married an Aussie, and he never saw or heard from her again.

My mum says he took to the drink and died of a broken heart."

Lorna motions for Jenny to stop. "Now, we need to find out who knew Simon Balding was allergic to wasps. Did he even know? I'm waiting to view his medical records. If he didn't know that a wasp sting could kill him then no one else would either – and that would include his father. If that is the case we can conclude the death was an accident."

*

Jenny and Jamal climb the last few stairs to reach Nigel Wang's tenement flat. The dentist lives in one of the more stunning 'wally closes' in Broomhill - from the entrance door through to the top landing, the lower portion of the walls are covered with small, white, square tiles topped and toed with a bottle green border tile incorporating, at intervals, an art nouveau design. The decorative tile could easily have been designed by Margaret Macdonald, the famous artist wife of Charles Rennie Mackintosh. A large stained glass window with a similar floral design illuminates the top landing providing pink and white speckles of light. The nameplate on the right-hand door is 'Wang'. As they approach they hear classical piano music coming from inside. After three knocks the music stops.

Nigel Wang opens the door and leads them through a long, spacious hall into an enormous living room filled with antique furniture and plants. In the corner bay window, taking pride of place in the room, is a shiny, black baby grand piano.

"Please, take a seat." Jenny chooses to sit on the chaise longue and Jamal on the deep red Chesterfield armchair. "Would you like a cup of something?"

"No, no thanks" responds Jamal, "We just need to ask you a few questions about your relationship with Simon Balding."

"It was an employee, employer relationship. We were not friends outside work. We had a professional relationship."

"Did you like him?" asks Jenny.

"I had nothing but respect for Simon Balding Senior, but I was not as impressed with his son. For a start, he had no respect for the arts, no appreciation of classical music. The only thing he respected was money."

"He made a lot more profit than his father, why was that?"

"I just did my job. I didn't ask questions. My wife lost her job as a music teacher going round schools so I would never do anything to jeopardize mine. No, now I must use my nimble fingers to practice dentistry."

Jenny keeps probing. "Simon must have been doing something differently from his father, if the business was going from strength to strength."

"I did notice a lot of middle-aged women in the reception area wearing braces, but we consult behind closed doors, so I've no idea what he was saying. I presume it was good advice. He just did more cosmetic work than his father." He looks upwards, "Culture is diminishing while vanity is rising."

"Not all dentists are doctors, is that right?" asks Jamal.

"That is right, what is confusing is that my doctorate is in music, not medicine."

Jenny is intrigued. "So, how did you end up a dentist in Scotland, Dr Wang?"

"I came to study piano at the Conservatoire in Glasgow. I fell in love with a cello player so here I am. Not many jobs in Scotland for concert pianists. Many jobs for dentists so I went back to school. Many people in Scotland have rotten teeth."

"That's true." Jenny tries to smile without showing any of her amalgam fillings.

"I first met Simon Balding Senior at one of my piano recitals in Pollok House. Now, that is an excellent piano. A Steinway."

Jamal shuffles in his seat. "Dr Wang… how long had you been hearing beeping in the surgery?"

"A couple of weeks."

"And why didn't you go up to the attic yourself?"

"Because it is not my surgery."

Jenny's phone rings. "Excuse me, Dr Wang, I'll have to take this." Jenny moves out into the hall which is adorned with musical themed paintings and photographs.

"Hi, Boss."

"Hi Jenny. That's Simon Balding's medical report in. He was stung by a wasp when he was fourteen, and hospitalized for two weeks. He very nearly died."

Jenny replies, "So he was aware another sting could be fatal."

"Yes, and that means his family also knew. Ask his colleague if he knew of the allergy."

"Okay, Boss."

"And note his reaction when you ask the question."

"Will do."

Jenny's eyes are drawn to a photograph of what must have been Nigel Wang, aged around ten, wearing a black suit, white shirt and bow tie, on a stage, sitting at a piano, with his little hands perched over the keys. She returns to deathly silence in the living room as Jamal has failed to keep the conversation going.

"Sorry about that." Jenny retakes her seat. "Do you have any more questions, Jamal?"

"No."

"I have just one." Jenny looks directly into the thirty-two-year-old's, kindly brown eyes. "Were you aware, Dr Wang, that Simon Balding Junior was allergic to wasps?"

"I had no idea. He didn't tell me. He only told me what I needed to know – like if something was being delivered to the surgery that required a signature – such as implants."

Jenny and Jamal enter a scruffy tenement close, in Kelvinbridge, and climb to the first floor, where Simon Balding's dental assistant, Rachel, lives with her parents. A young man, hiding behind a beard, answers the door wearing only a pair of jeans. It's 2pm and it looks like he's just woken up. However, his eyes wake up sharply when the two police detectives show their ID.

"We just want to ask your sister a few questions."

"Rachel? She's not my sister, she's my girlfriend." He shouts, "Rach!"

A faint voice replies, "I'm not dressed. I'll be through in a minute."

Returning his gaze to the detectives he says, "You'd better come in. You can wait in the kitchen."

Jenny and Jamal stand awkwardly in the small, cramped room, waiting for Rachel to appear, trying not to brush their clothes against any of the dirty dishes strewn all over the worktop.

Jenny breaks the ice. "Parents on holiday?"

"Benidorm."

"Nice."

"She won't let anyone see her without her makeup". Rachel's bearded boyfriend reaches up to a cupboard door. "Want a drink of juice?"

They answer in unison, "No thanks."

Rachel enters the room tucking a t-shirt that says, 'Guilty!' on it into her jeans.

"So, you admit, you're guilty," jokes Jenny.

Rachel's eyes narrow.

"Your t-shirt says so."

Rachel smirks.

"We just want to ask you a few routine questions about your job at the dental practice. Nothing to worry about."

As the boyfriend leaves the room he says, "Is that what the polis said to Robert McTavish before youse beat a confession out of him?" He pauses in the doorway, "I saw that programme about miscarriages of justice. Shocking, so it was." As he enters another room his voice fades. His parting line is, "Tell them nothing Rach."

With her confidant gone, Jenny turns to face Rachel. "Did you like working for Simon Balding?"

"It was all right."

"Did you have a good relationship?"

"Yeh."

"Then why were you applying for jobs elsewhere?"

Rachel's voice rises. "Who telt you that?"

Jamal explains, "A month ago you uploaded a cv to a job site."

"So what if I did? The pay's lousy."

Jenny asks, "Is it true you encouraged Mr Balding to go up to the attic?"

"Look, it wiznae just me harpin' on aboot the bleepin'. Dr Wang telt him too. It wasnae ma fault he went up to the attic. I didnae know he wiz allergic."

*

The dental receptionist places her hand over the mouthpiece of the landline phone and says, quietly, "I'll be with you in a minute." Jenny and Jamal take a seat in the stylish waiting area which could easily belong to one of Glasgow's top hair salons. Designer plastic yellow seats are fixed together in rows to form a square. Large, leafy plants have been positioned in each corner to make it feel less regimented and at intervals a little spray of citrus air freshener is released into the atmosphere.

A selection of magazines are scattered on low glossy white tables. Everything is glossy. The photographs on the covers of the magazines show healthy, smiling people showing off their perfect teeth - images which have likely been further enhanced using computer software.

Providing calming entertainment in the waiting area is a fabulous tropical fish tank set into the wall. Jamal and Jenny watch mesmerized as orange and white stripy fish swim around the crystal clear water occasionally dodging groups of smaller, glowing electric blue fish, each with a flash of red in its tail. The tank is illuminated by subtle artificial lighting hidden amongst green vegetation and coral.

The chatty receptionist is talking on the phone. "I'm afraid I don't yet know what's happening with the surgery. At the moment I can only make appointments to see Dr Wang." She covers the mouthpiece and looks in the direction of the detectives and mouths the word, "Obviously." She listens some more then replaces the receiver. "How come I'm the only one around here who has to keep working? How come I'm the one who has to feed the fish?"

Jenny and Jamal move over to the reception desk to begin the interview. Jamal asks the first question. "Who are you taking these instructions from Miss Wilson?"

"Mrs Balding, Simon's mother. She called me on Tuesday and asked me to come back to work today. She said Dr Wang will return to work next Monday and if any of Simon's patients phone she told me to tell them she's looking for a locum dentist to take over Simon's workload as soon as possible. She doesn't yet know what they are going to do with the surgery. Well, that's what she told me anyway."

"What do you think will happen?" asks Jenny.

"I reckon she'll sell it, now there are no dentists left in the family. And to think not long ago they had two with the same name."

"Miss Wilson, did you like Simon Balding Junior?"

She studies her newly applied nail varnish. "He was all right. A bit of a womanizer, mind. He had it off with someone …" She points at the open door of Simon's Balding's consulting room. The reclining dentist's chair is visible, "…right there on that chair."

"How do you know that?" asks Jenny who enjoys a bit of gossip.

"Because, his fiancé caught him at it."

"Bryony Jenkins?"

"No. The last one. Her name was Kirstin. They look quite similar though."

"And how do you know all this?"

"Glasgow's a small place. My friend Megan plays badminton with her brother in the churches league. He was all for beating him up, but Kirstin begged him not to. She wanted to beat him up hersel."

"And did she?"

"No!" A cuckoo appears 5 times from inside a box above the receptionists head. "Another Verbier purchase," she says, sneeringly, then picks up a small Tupperware box and asks, "Do you mind if I feed the fish while we continue talking? I don't want to be late to pick up the little yin."

"No, please go ahead."

She pulls out a three-step ladder from under the counter and moves it over to the wall housing the fish tank.

"Have you dealt with many angry customers since Simon Balding Junior took over the surgery, Ms Wilson?"

She climbs the three steps and carefully slides open the lid of the fish tank. "Lots. Mostly about money. A perfect smile doesn't come cheap if ye eat sweets."

"Any threats?"

She smiles as she takes out the little tub of fish food from her pocket, "Just the girlfriend."

"Another one?"

"Yip. Now *she* was the best looking one of the lot. She was called Sophie." Taking some flakes from the tub and dropping them into the tank she adds, "Sophie was a model."

Jenny studies a smiling photograph of Simon Balding hanging on the wall in the reception area. In all fairness he does look better than after the wasp attack, but, with a polished, bald head and beady light-blue eyes, not significantly better. She wonders how a guy who looked like this at such a young age could pull such good-looking women.

The receptionist closes the tank and returns to the floor. "Sophie went totally raj."

"Raj?"

"Mental."

"I don't know what he'd done wrong. She most probably caught him cheating."

"But you don't know?"

"Leopards don't change their spots." She flicks a switch at the side of the fish tank. The lights in the tank go out. "Night night little fishies. See you in the morning."

Jamal asks, "Do you know where Sophie lives now?"

"I wouldn't know, but she was really pally with Simon's sister Ruby. They went to uni together. She was with her at the time of the accident."

TWO YEARS EARLIER

The rain comes down in torrents, bouncing off the roads, making the hilly streets in Glasgow's West End even more treacherous than normal. Although it rains almost every second day in Glasgow, it rarely rains with this ferocity and the River Kelvin is close to bursting its banks.

Ruby cycles along Oakfield Avenue and turns right into Great Western Road just as the traffic lights turn to amber. Her friend Sophie, cycling behind her, approaches just at the lights switch to red. She pedals faster to make it through the lights, then, at the last moment, changes her mind and instinctively pulls on both brakes. The bike skids, Sophie is thrown from the saddle, over the handlebars and onto the road.

A brave pedestrian rushes over to help the motionless cyclist. Another pedestrian darts onto the road to remove the bicycle. A dazed Sophie opens her eyes and becoming aware of lights, driving rain and traffic noises makes an effort to rise. She is helped up by the middle-aged man wearing a pinstripe suit. "Are you hurt?"

"I..." She feels her legs. "I... don't think so."

He helps her to the side of the road. "That was a close one. You could have ended up under a lorry. If that lorry had turned left..."

"I hit the brakes..."

"Sorry, I've got to go." He rushes along the pavement in the direction of Kelvinbridge

Underground holding a briefcase over his head and leaves a shaken Sophie behind to cope by herself.

Cars and vans had begun swerving past the fallen cyclist almost immediately. Pedestrians, drivers, everyone is in a hurry tonight as Scotland are playing Slovakia at Hampden. Kick off's in half-an-hour. It's why the girls were heading into the city centre – to watch the match with their friends in a sports' bar in West Nile Street.

Sophie covers her mouth with her hand, then pulls it away to view a hand now stained with blood.

Ruby, having made it through the lights, was well beyond Kelvinbridge before she realised her friend was not directly behind her. She cycles back to find her friend sobbing and grappling with a mangled bike.

"Sophie. Are you alright?"

"No!" She covers her bloody mouth.

"My mouth… My teeth…"

"What happened?"

Crying now, slightly hysterically, Sophie explains what happened and how she could have ended up much worse off – she could have been hit by a lorry or bus.

Ruby states, "We'll go straight to accident and emergency."

They padlock their bikes against the nearest lamppost. Sophie unclips her cycling helmet and moves her hand slowly across her forehead.

"Oh my God, I can feel a lump."

Ruby examines it and tries to reassure her. "You seem to be understanding everything that's going on though."

"What d'you mean?"

"Well, your brain seems to be working okay." Ruby waves down a black cab. They climb into the back seat. However, when the driver notices in his rear view mirror that Sophie is injured as well as drenched, he unlocks his seatbelt, steps out of the car and opens the back door for a better look.

"You'd better no' get ony blood on my interior. I paid an extra grand to get the tartan wool mix."

He moves round to the boot, opens it, takes out a towel and hands it through the window to Sophie. "That'll help."

Ruby can't believe his callousness. "Can you take us to the nearest Accident and Emergency? Do you know where that is?"

"Naw."

"Do you know where the Glasgow Royal Infirmary is?"

He steps back into the driver's seat. "Obviously." He seems narked. "What way d'you want to go?"

"I don't know. You're the taxi driver."

"I think, at this time of day, going round the M8 would be quickest."

"Go that way then. My friend has just fallen off her bike, although you seem more concerned about your bloody tartan."

"Now, now. There's no need for that kind o' language."

The two girls pass through electronic doors in the bowels of the hospital. They follow the signs for Accident and Emergency. At the end of the corridor, they enter a huge room with rows of seats and lots of unhealthy-looking people sitting on them. A woman, who impatiently overtook them in the corridor, makes a dash for the reception desk and pulls a number from a machine issuing tickets. They do likewise and take a seat. The number they have drawn is 157. A 'Now serving' electronic display switches from '125' to '126'.

Ruby says, "I wonder how long it'll take to see thirty-one people? That's how many's before us." She looks at her watch. "That's the match started."

Sophie says in a self-pitying tone, "I couldn't care less about the match. I could lose my teeth. I remember a girl at High School didn't wear a gum shield and lost two front teeth when she was hit in the face by a hockey ball."

"Let's just wait and see what they say. You might be lucky."

Sophie rubs her forehead. "I can feel a huge lump now. And it's growing."

Ruby moves her hand over the hard, raised bulge on her friend's forehead. "As long as you can see and you're brain isn't affected. That's all that really matters, Sophie."

"But, what about my modelling jobs?"

"You can still model with a couple of false teeth and remember that's the worse case scenario. I bet half the super-models out there have a few falsers."

"You reckon? Oh, I'd better call Freda and let her know what's happened."

Sophie struggles to take out a mobile phone from a front pocket in her tight, wet jeans. The screen is smashed to smithereens.

"Oh no. How much is that going to cost me?"

"Sophie. It's just a possession. These things can be replaced. What can't be replaced is you."

"Oh, thanks Ruby." She touches her friend's arm, sniffles then adds, "I don't know what I'd do without you." Aware the electronic number on the wall hasn't changed in a while she adds, "I think we're in for a long wait."

"Can you look to the left. Good. Now the right. Good. Up and down. Good. Can you read that sign over there?"

Sophie reads the sign."**Please do not abuse our staff**."

The young female doctor concludes, "That's fine, your eye-sight seems to be okay. The swelling on your forehead must have been caused by your helmet jarring against it when you hit the ground." Sophie nods in agreement. "But I believe your cycling helmet has prevented a serious head injury. If you hadn't been wearing it, you'd be in intensive care right now."

Sophie releases air from her mouth when she imagines what might have been, how close she came to a very different outcome.

"But, I warn you, that bruising will turn to black and blue. By tomorrow you'll look like you've lost a fight."

"How long will it take to heal, Doctor?"

"A few weeks, but if the pain gets any worse in the night don't hesitate to phone the NHS 24 helpline." She passes her a piece of paper with the number.

"Thanks."

"Now, we've cleaned your mouth, but your front two teeth have moved forward a bit so you'll have to go straight away to see a dentist. Are you registered with one?"

"Only at home, in Campbeltown. I'm a student here."

"In that case you'll need to go first thing in the morning to the dental hospital on Sauchiehall Street. D'you know where it is?"

Ruby responds, "I know where it is. I'll take you, Sophie. It's near Charing Cross."

"Her brother's a dentist," adds Sophie by way of an explanation.

"It opens at 8am. Go as early as possible."

"Thank you, Doctor. Thank you so much."

Leaving the hospital, they pass a drunk man happily staggering about a corridor singing lyrics from the old James Bond movie *From Russia with Love*. As they pass him, he bends his knees and pretends to point a gun at them and, with one arm outstretched, makes a pretend-sound of firing it. They presume Scotland must be one step closer to qualifying for Russia 2018.

*

Sophie has a restless night, tossing and turning. She had assured her mother on the phone that she was all right but now she's not so sure. Her forehead is throbbing and every time she touches it she imagines the lump is growing. One eye is becoming increasingly hard to open. She reminds herself that things always seem worse in the middle of the night. The morning should bring a more optimistic perspective.

At 7am she rises, looks in the mirror and screams. She sees the reflection of a battered woman.

Her flatmate Vanessa runs in from the adjacent room and turns on the light.

"What the hell?" Vanessa stares a Sophie's black eye. The eye is half-shut. Accustomed to seeing her flatmate with silky, clear, unblemished skin and near perfect features, the transformation is truly shocking.

Vanessa waves her hands in front of Sophie's face. "Can you see me?"

Calming down a bit Sophie replies, "I can see the daft rollers in your hair."

Her flatmate feels her own head, "Oh, yeh I forgot I had them in."

The doorbell rings.

"That'll be Ruby," says Sophie.

On route to the dental hospital, Sophie is reminded how dreadful she looks when people stare at her and grimace. She tries to convince fellow travellers, the bus driver and a woman walking a cute Dachshund, that she hasn't just been beaten up by her boyfriend. "I don't even have a boyfriend," she repeats over and over. Ruby concurs, but no one seems to believe them. They alight at Woodlands Road near Charing Cross and cross the roaring motorway along with a throng of pedestrians heading to their respective places of work.

Ruby points in the direction of Renfrew Street. "We go left up this street."

"I've never been up here before." The two girls begin the gradual climb. "Some of the buildings are quite black aren't they?"

"Probably just need sand-blasted. The Dental School's on the right somewhere further up. I looked it up on Google Street View. It's quite an attractive building on the Renfrew Street side."

They reach an entrance which has 'INCORPORATED DENTAL HOSPITAL' carved in stone above the door.

"This is it, Sophie. I can't believe how different it looks compared to the other side."

"What does the other side look like?"

"Really ugly."

The young women sit down on the stone steps and wait for the building to open.

"So, you fell off your bike, did you?" It would seem the dentist treating Sophie doesn't believe her either. She makes a mental note to buy an eye patch, or to stay indoors for a month.

"Yes, I fell off my bike yesterday in Great Western Road. I didn't think I'd need witnesses to prove it."

"Okay. Open nice and wide." He shines a light inside her mouth focusing on the back of her front two teeth. "Your teeth have moved a fraction so we'll have to freeze your mouth and try to realign them, but first we'll have to do an x-ray."

Ruby sits in the waiting room as Sophie returns occasionally to tell her where she is off to next. She has watched patients come and go for hours and read every sign, and is now so bored she has begun reading lecture notes.

Sophie taps her on the shoulder.

"That's me finished."

"Oh good."

"Sophie smiles to show her temporary brace."

"Wow, thank goodness you could come here Soph. Imagine what this would be costing if you had to pay for it privately."

"I've to come back in three weeks to have it removed."

"So, you're not going to lose them then?"

"He says it's too early to tell. They don't really know yet, but if they hadn't moved them back today I would have lost them for certain. Apparently you only have a 48-hour window to realign them or they would have set that way. And the sooner they're moved, the better chance they have of healing."

"Lucky we didn't muck about then," replies Ruby thankful the traumatic event has had a satisfactory ending. "Fancy pie, beans and chips at The Griffin to celebrate?"

Sophie opens her mouth and points to her brace. "What, with this on?"

"You can have some liquidized soup or something. And we can sneak you in one of the booths so no one sees you."

"Nobody will believe me when I tell them I'm a part-time model."

Ruby links her friend's arm as they walk the short distance along Sauchiehall Street. "Yes, they would. You're tall and slim and imagine how much weight you'll lose in three weeks if you can't eat proper food. You see, Sophie, there is always a silver lining."

*

After recuperating for more than a week at her parents' modest home in Campbeltown, Sophie returns to Glasgow, making the four-hour, tedious, road trip by bus. Back in her student digs, she continues to lie low until the brace has been removed and the mottled blue marks around her sparkling green eyes have disappeared altogether.

Returning to the Dental Hospital this time, Ruby goes into the consultation room with her to listen to the final prognosis because the last time Sophie didn't seem to understand all of the dental jargon.

The dentist removes the wire which held the brace together and pulls off the bits of plastic glued to Sophie's teeth.

"You like the colour blue?" The dentist is commenting on Ruby's blue hair, piercing blue eyes, blue eyeshadow and electric blue eyeliner. Today she is even wearing dark blue lipstick. He offers Sophie a hand held mirror.

"My hair colour is 'denim' actually'."

Sophie, sitting up, studies her teeth in the mirror.

The dentist's focus returns to his patient. "So far your teeth have healed reasonably well Miss Stewart, but we don't know what the future holds. However, we can't continue to treat you here at the dental hospital."

This is not welcome news to Sophie who worries about the cost of everything.

"You'll have to register with a dentist. I can give you a list away with you if you want."

"Honestly there's no need."

Ruby pipes up, "My brother's a dentist. He has a dental practice in the Merchant City."

"Well, someone needs to monitor your teeth every few months because it's likely you'll need, at the very least, to have root canal treatment."

*

They catch the underground from Byres Road to Buchanan Street and walk through George Square towards the Merchant City. They pass an impressive five-storey high mural depicting badminton players on the side of a brick building, painted to celebrate the 2014 Commonwealth Games. Sophie is too busy looking at the ground to notice.

"Ruby, I thought you didn't like your brother?"

"I don't much, but I think he's a good dentist, he was top of his class at Newcastle, and he may give you a discount. I know my dad would have."

They pass a café and, on seeing them, a worker hastily turns the sign on the door from 'Open' to 'Closed'.

"Didn't you fall out with him at your Dad's funeral."

"Families like mine do that kind of thing then make up. He was friendly enough when I sent the texts about you."

"That's a relief."

"My dad bought the shop in this area because that was his favourite pub." A group of office workers dart across the road and disappear into Rab Ha's public house.

They turn the corner and arrive at a glass-fronted shop in Glassford Street, just as Simon Balding is finishing up for the day. The door is locked. Ruby rings the door bell.

"I hope he hasn't gone home."

When Simon Balding sees his sister through the glass, he hurries to open the door.

"If it isn't my annoying sister. Come in, come in." Once they're inside, he throws his thickset arms around Ruby in a phony kind of way and turns to look at Sophie. "And who is this – beauty?"

"Simon!"

"Sorry."

"This is my highly intelligent friend, Sophie, who I told you about in my texts. The one who fell off her bike and smashed her teeth."

"Okay, okay so you've already been to the dental hospital so you won't need any treatment right now. Why don't I take a quick look at your teeth then we nip over to Rab Ha's. I've had a hard day. Being nice to the general public takes its toll."

*

Three months later Sophie sits on the edge of the dentist's chair about to have her teeth examined again by Simon Balding. "Can you remind me what they said again at the dental hospital?"

"The dentist there said I might need root canal treatment," replies Sophie.

"That's true. Sometimes, root canal treatment can work."

"They haven't felt too sore."

"That's good, now open wide."

Simon Balding leans over and using metal implements fishes around inside her mouth.

"A few amalgam fillings need replaced I see. He tugs at her front teeth."

"Ahhh!"

"Was that sore?"

Sophie struggles to say, "A bit."

He withdraws his implements and rolls off his plastic gloves.

He hums and haws and screws up his face.

She asks, "What is it?"

"You could spend money on root canal treatment, but in my opinion it would be a waste."

Sophie swings her legs off the chair. "Why?"

"...because it's quite a long, painful procedure and it looks very much like they are going to rot over time and you'll end up needing implants..."

"Implants?"

"Yes, your two front teeth will eventually die and they'll need to be replaced with something else."

"Something else?"

"Can you not see they are slightly discoloured already?"

He pushes a mirror closer to Sophie's face to allow her to see.

"You know I hadn't noticed."

"If you can't afford implants which are roughly £4,000 each, the only option on the NHS is to have a plate fitted."

An image flashes through Sophie's mind of her Gran's false teeth soaking in a glass of water.

"The implant option would feel no different from how they do now and would last a life-time."

"I can't believe it – the dental hospital talked about root-canal treatment."

"Yes, but as you said yourself, they had no idea how your teeth would heal over time. Adult teeth never heal as well as childrens'. I'm afraid yours haven't fully recovered from the trauma, and they will definitely blacken over time as they die."

"I can't do modelling with black teeth."

"That's why the implant option would be the ideal solution for you, Sophie, as they'd look exactly like your original teeth. I'd make sure of that. I'm one of the more experienced implant surgeons in Scotland, despite my age, because of what I learned during my time in Harley Street."

Sophie covers her face with both hands and make some faint, animal-like noises.

"I know it's not good news and I know you're a student. Since you're Ruby's friend I could give you a 10% discount."

Her hands move to her cheeks. "I'll need to get a bank loan."

"Remember, the NHS option is available free of charge. It makes no difference to me which option you go for. People get used to having plates in their mouths. It's not that bad."

"Would you want one?"

"Obviously I would choose the implants. Who wouldn't if they could afford them."

*

Sophie lies on her bed listening to melancholy music to match her low mood. She has just come off the phone to her mother, who, although sympathetic, is unable to offer her much help money wise. Her exact words were, "your father and I could maybe scrape together £1,000 or so if we both do a lot of overtime". Since Sophie needs £7,200 even with the 10% discount, this contribution is a drop in the ocean. Prior to calling her mum, Sophie made an appointment with her bank manager. If they'll lend her the money she has already decided to go ahead with the implants.

"She's coming round," observes Simon Balding's dental assistant.

Simon finishes booking two seats for the play *Candlelight* at the Theatre Royal and selects an option on his computer to collect the tickets at the box office.

Simon hands over a mirror.

"Don't be too shocked."

Sophie opens her eyes to a slit to view the ghastly sight of her toothless self. She now has a large gap right in the middle of her front teeth.

"Oh, horrible. I'm so ugly. I'll be staying at home as much as possible until you can replace them."

"The two months will pass in no time, you'll see. You can do plenty of studying while your gums heal."

"I certainly won't be going anywhere near the student union."

Simon reaches for her leather jacket. "Make an appointment at reception in one month's time so I can check your gums are healing okay." He helps her on with her jacket. "They need to heal properly before the implants can be fitted."

"I know, Simon. It's just hard to get my head around not having my front teeth when I never had any problems with them at all before the accident."

On entering her student flat, after her minor operation, feeling very sorry for herself, Sophie picks up the landline to find out if her mum has called while she was out. The different dial tone signals someone has left a message. A woman's voice says, 'First new message, received today at 4:30.' She hears the familiar voice belonging to her mother. Normally happy to be living in Glasgow, she is suddenly struck by how far away from home she is, how far she is from crying into her mother's arms.

"Mum, here. Hope you're okay, Honey. Remember I love you even if you are toothless. I'll try you again later when I get home from work." The message ends and then the bland recorded voice returns, 'Next new message received today at 5:20. It turns out to be a voice she hasn't heard in months."

"I've got amazing news, Sophie. Helen Fountaine has been in contact again, you know the head of advertising at Mariel Cosmetics, the one I spoke about when you signed up with the agency. Well, she has chosen your face Sophie to be the new face of Mariel Cosmetics. Can you believe it?"

Facing a mirror above the hall table Sophie looks into it and opens her mouth, making visible the large gap in the centre of her teeth.

"And to think you worried about spending money on those fabulous photos for your portfolio. Helen *loved* them. Loves you. Says you are absolutely perfect. Just what she's looking for."

Still clutching the phone, Sophie stares at herself in the mirror. "The contract is for two years so you'll have to postpone your studies. Call me when you hear this message. Just think, in no time you'll be able to replace that rusty old bike with a brand new sports car... if that's what you want. Bye for now... And, oh... It couldn't have happened to a nicer girl... Well done... Speak soon. Byeeeee!"

*

"I can't put the implants in now."

Sophie stands defiantly in Simon Balding's consulting room having barged into the surgery without an appointment.

"The company can't wait two months. The contract's worth £100,000. Please put the implants in now, Simon. I'm begging you?"

"I'm sorry, but I can't put patient safety at risk."

"I'll sign something. Do anything."

"Honestly, I can't, Sophie. I'm sorry, but nothing can be done until your gums have healed. It's just unfortunate the timing of the offer."

"You're telling me!"

"But you can't blame me. You're teeth would have blackened over time. Now if you don't mind, Sophie, I have a patient in pain waiting to see me."

The door of Simon Balding's room flies open and Sophie Stewart marches out, passed the reception area where a man sits holding his hand against his jaw. Out in the street, she covers her head with her hands and lets out an almighty scream.

THE INVESTIGATION CONTINUES

"We need to interview this… Sophie Stewart. We need to find out why the relationship turned sour."

"Do you have an address for her yet, Jamal?"

"I'll email it to you."

"No, Jamal. I want you to hand it to me on a piece of paper. I refuse to live my life like the rest of you – staring at a computer screen all day long. It's very unhealthy."

"Sophie Stewart is back living with her parents in Campbeltown, Boss. She graduated this year with a 2:1 in Philosophy from Glasgow University." Jamal has done his homework.

"So she's smart."

"Yes, but not as smart as Ruby Balding who received a 1st. But that wasn't her first degree. She already had a degree in Art History."

"How come some folk spend half their lives being students?" asks Alistair. "I was skint enough after one degree."

Jenny pipes up, "Almost all my friends from uni have ended up back home living with their parents."

"How interesting, Jenny." Lorna takes a sip of green tea. "Now, do you fancy a trip to Campbeltown?"

"Oh that'd be great," responds Jenny enthusiastically.

"You can go there with Alistair." Alistair's eyes light up. "Because I'm sure you'd like to take a look at the famous Machrihanish Links. Am I right, Alistair?"

"Wouldn't have time to play the golf course. It's an eight hour round trip by car."

"Yes, but it's not by plane." DI Gunn smiles as she delivers the good news. "Would you believe the flight takes only 11 mins from Glasgow airport?"

"11 minutes!"

"Yip. A saving of seven hours and thirty-eight minutes."

She looks at Jenny, "Would you have needed a calculator to work that out?"

"I'm not that bad, Boss."

"I'll take your word for it. By all means Alistair, take your clubs. This case should be wrapped up soon. Jenny can do some sight-seeing. I believe it has the oldest cinema in Scotland and you can also look out for a bronze statue of Linda McCartney holding a little lamb."

Jenny turns to Jamal shrugging her shoulders.

"Sir Paul McCartney's first wife who sadly died." Lorna looks away and gazes upwards, smiling. "I loved that song Mull of Kintyre and the video of the pipe band marching along Saddell beach..." Lorna laughs, "Then Linda appears wearing a pair of wellies carrying a baby."

"Can we go now, Boss?" Alistair has booked a lunchtime lesson with a golf pro.

"Golf lesson, Alistair?"

He picks up a long parcel from under his desk. "You know me too well, Boss."

"Bought another driver on Ebay, have we?"

"Don't tell Susie, she's on my case enough as it is. At least I'm buying second-hand stuff."

Lorna taps her nose, "Don't worry Alistair your secret's safe with me."

*

"Was one leg longer than the other?"

"Colin! Of course it wasn't."

"No need to be so touchy, Lorna."

"Drawing figures, it's not as easy as you'd think. And I'm certain she moved."

"So, it's a she?"

"Yes, and quite young. I ended up with a side-on view this time."

"Did you learn another technique?"

"Yes, it was great. It's called the 'gesture drawing method'. I'll have to show it to Daisy, as I think it would really help her draw characters quickly for her computer games programmes."

"How does it work then?"

Lorna flips to a previous page in her drawing pad and points to three quickly drawn line sketches. "You start by drawing simple shapes for the head, torso and pelvis, followed by the limbs and joints and then you draw a single line through them. You can see a line of action. Here she's doing a ballet pose.

"I wonder if Degas used the technique?"

"Probably, cause he worked fast. In this drawing can you tell she's crouching?"

"I think so."

"In this one she's about to stab someone."

Colin takes a sip of Black Bottle, his favourite blended whisky, which he's been drinking a bit too much of since he found out his beloved library is threatened with closure along with his job. "And how's the case going?"

"Quite well. It's such a relief, for once, not having to fend off the press day and night. I think we're all enjoying doing things outside work for a change. Jenny was encouraging me to go to the Cupar Arts Festival when we visit Dundee. It's not too far away. She's already been with her architect boyfriend. I think he's from that area. She thought it was brilliant. They saw some artist's light show at the top of a disused sugar silo. Said it was great."

"Sounds ambitious."

"Very. And I've been doing my own research on what's worth visiting in Dundee. According to Daisy it's the new tourist capital of Scotland." She takes a sip of wine. "I do miss her Colin, don't you?"

Colin nods, sips his whisky. He has tears in his eyes. His daughter doesn't need him anymore and neither do his employers. Earlier in the evening he had looked up the definition of 'redundant' in the dictionary. There was a long list of words he could use to describe himself; 'Redundant, adjective: no longer needed or useful. Synonyms: unnecessary, not required, inessential, unessential, needless, unneeded, dispensable, disposable, expendable, unwanted, useless.' Yes, he thought morosely, the words described him perfectly.

*

As she polishes her precious money plant Lorna's thoughts turn to Colin and all the dedicated librarians out there. Speaking to the plant, she says, "Now is the time to pay out. Just keep these libraries open and I promise I won't throw you out of the window."

Alistair comes down the corridor and pauses at her open door. "I'll call back later when you're alone."

"I *am* alone, Alistair. I was talking to my money plant."

"It's proved to be a bit of a dud, hasn't it, Boss? Are you sure you've got it in the right position?"

"Yes. The guy who took the Feng Shui night class told me to put it in the north-west corner of my desk."

"Maybe it's just a load of rubbish."

Lorna ignores the remark. "Alistair, about this case. Don't you think it odd that Ruby Balding was staying in a private flat in Glasgow?"

He leans against the door frame hiding a putter behind his back. "Yeh, I've thought of that. Why wasn't she living at home? It's even in the West End."

Lorna pours a little water into her plant. "The most likely reason is she had fallen out with her father or mother or both."

"Maybe she didn't get on with her step-mother?"

"Step-mother?"

"Yeh, Jamal found birth certificates online which prove Simon and Ruby were half brother and sister. They had different mothers. He also found Ruby's mother's death certificate – seems she died in a road accident."

"Oh dear, but great work on Jamal's part. What would we do with out him?"

"It wasn't so long ago you were threatening to send Technie Jamal to the cyber hub in Edinburgh."

She smiles, "We all make mistakes, but only intelligent people learn from them."

Alistair continues onto the next room and enters his own office. Lorna hears the door close gently. A few moments later she hears a tapping sound followed by a ball rolling across the floor. The golf-obsessed detective is practising putting into his waste paper basket in preparation for tonight's match.

*

An upside down wooden placard rests against a tree. On the ground lies a pile of similar placards with different messages pasted on the boards. Colin stands surrounded by a large group of people on Glasgow Green. The signs say, 'End of civilisation.' 'Hands off our libraries.' 'Dicken's world returns.' And Colin's personal favourite 'Bankers cooked the books not us.'

"We've been told to wait here until the organisers give us the go-ahead. Libraries are off last, after post office workers and community centres. The turn out is much higher than expected so we've been warned it could be a 30 minute wait until we set off."

Colin spots two people waving at him from the direction of the People's Palace. As they near he recognises his wife Lorna and their daughter Daisy. They are carrying three cups of coffee.

Twenty minutes into the march, half way up Bath Street, Colin turns round and looks back down the hill at the marching crowds behind him chanting and waving banners. He is reminded of that brilliant sunny January day, fifteen years earlier, when he and his pals, marched on this same route against the war in Iraq. That was a rousing sight he would never forget. Lorna was a new recruit at the time and he remembers winking at her in her police uniform as he passed by. They had all felt a sense of anger mixed with hope that day yet, in the end, millions of people protesting across the UK were ignored. He desperately hoped this protest would have a different outcome.

*

As Alistair gazes through the small aeroplane window at the squiggly landmass below that is the Mull of Kintyre, Jenny stares, white faced, at a fixed point in the interior of the cabin, trying desperately not to be sick. It has only taken nine minutes for her to feel this bad.

The pilot announces, in an English accent, for the cabin crew to prepare for landing. Sighs are released from all the passengers with a less than sturdy constitution, as the single crew member takes his seat facing the two detectives.

"This is great, isn't it?" Jenny says nothing. Her face is ashen. Alistair gapes wide eyed at the Machrihanish sand dunes and the huge areas of sweeping greenery bordering the Atlantic Ocean. As the plane begins to descend, he can make out the fairways and greens of the famous links golf course.

Jenny's voice is weak. "How did you get on last night?"

"I was beaten by a fourteen-year-old who didn't even play well."

The wheels of the plane whirr into position. Bump, bump, bump, bump. They travel a hundred yards along a runway and come to an abrupt stop. As the passengers reach for their belongings and leave the small blue and white plane, the song 'Mull of Kintyre' plays through the cabin speakers.

Once inside the terminal, they take a seat and wait for Jenny to recover.

"I thought you'd be used to travelling in shoogly planes and over rough seas coming from Stornoway."

"Well, you thought wrong, Alistair."

"So the plan is we interview Sophie Stewart. That shouldn't take long as she's working here in Machrihanish. Then you can take the shuttle bus into Campbeltown if you want and I'll play a round of golf. We'll meet in the clubhouse at 5 o'clock."

"Fine."

"You don't sound fine."

"I'm starting to feel better now." She stands up, "Now, let's hit the action in Machrihanish."

Two uniformed chambermaids appear in the corridor of the Machrihanish Hotel having completed the makeover of the last room on their shift which began at seven in the morning. The younger of the two steers a trolley, brimming with towels and sheets.

The two detectives approach. "Is either of you Sophie Stewart?" asks Alistair out of politeness knowing full well the small, dumpy, middle-aged woman with thinning, permed hair is unlikely to be on the books of any modelling agency.

"I am," replies Sophie who, in her current black and white chambermaid attire, would not be out of place in one of those period dramas on television.

Sophie collapses into a tartan upholstered armchair. Alistair and Jenny have been drinking coffee and eating scones with jam and clotted cream, and listening to piped Scottish music while waiting for her to finish work.

"I'm worn out," she announces.

"I'm not surprised," responds Jenny who always manages to say something to make interviewees feel at ease.

Sophie sits facing a large bay window overlooking the starter's hut and beyond it the blue Atlantic Ocean. Ireland, although not visible, is only twenty-one miles across the sea. Rays of warm sunlight filter through the glass, highlighting the freckles on Sophie's pale, blemish free, translucent skin and lighting up her emerald green eyes. Her long, straight, auburn hair has been scraped back and held in a messy bun. Alistair can't take his eyes off her.

"Is this about the house robbery? I already told them at Campbeltown Police Station, I didn't see the guy's face."

"No, this is about the death of Simon Balding."

"What's that got to do with me?" She rubs an ear, nervously. "You've come all the way here to ask me about *him*?"

Alistair asks, "I believe at one time you were in a relationship with Mr Balding..."

"Not true. He asked me out the first time I met him. We were all a bit drunk. I said no. I was never in a relationship with Simon Balding other than a dentist/patient relationship."

"Oh, I apologise."

Jenny asks, "Sophie, did you know Simon Balding was allergic to wasps?"

She looks puzzled. "No."

"Perhaps his sister told you?"

Sophie shakes her head. "No, Ruby didn't tell me that." She smiles, "but it *is* funny that it was tiny little wasps that got the better of him."

Alistair reprimands her. "You think this is funny?"

Sophie's smile drops. "I mean funny peculiar, not funny ha ha."

A red Porsche pulls into the car park and stops outside the bay window. Sophie says, sarcastically, "In these days of austerity, we all have to tighten our belts."

"You seem quite angry, Ms Stewart. Were you angry with Simon Balding?"

"I was, but, if you excuse the wasp analogy, 'Anger is a stone cast into a wasps' nest'."

"What does that mean?"

"It's an Indian proverb my Grandad used to use all the time, usually when my mum was taking a tantrum at him for not doing any housework. It means be careful where to use your anger because once you stir up trouble it sometimes cannot be stopped."

"Do you stir up trouble?" asks Jenny.

"Only when it's necessary."

"Why were you so angry with Simon Balding? The receptionist said you made quite a scene in the surgery."

"Simon was very keen to pull out my front two teeth after the cycling accident. Now I wish I'd had a second opinion."

"But you don't know what that opinion would have been?"

"Sure, but since then I've been told by an oral surgeon from Leeds, who comes here every year to play golf, that everyone is entitled to a second opinion from a consultant at a Dental Hospital."

"But you'd already been there, hadn't you?"

"Months earlier. Simon did not tell me my rights – that I was entitled to a second opinion at that point in time. He should have told me. The outcome might have been the same but, at least then I would have known for sure there was no other option available."

Jenny makes a mental note to seek a second opinion if her dentist ever suggests anything so drastic.

Sophie continues, "And, when I had a horrific space in the middle of my front teeth, one of the biggest cosmetic companies in France chose me to model their new range of skin care products. Can you believe that? Can you believe my bad luck?"

"Could they not have waited for your teeth to be sorted?" asks Jenny.

"No, they couldn't wait two months." Sophie adds sarcastically, "unsurprisingly."

"Is that why you tried to sue him?"

"I didn't get very far with that one. The lawyer I went to was very pessimistic about my chances of winning and refused to take it on a 'no win no fee' basis. I was already in too much debt to consider paying for it myself."

"Why didn't you go to an NHS dentist to have the dental work done for free if you were so hard up?"

"I did. He *was* an NHS dentist, but the NHS won't pay for implants."

"Are you still friendly with Ruby Balding?"

"I see her when I'm up in Glasgow. I think she feels sorry for me. That's why she's invited me to go to Verbier with her and her friends in December."

"Can you ski?" asks Alistair who is a keen snow-boarder.

"No, I've never been skiing in my life. Ruby says she'll pay for me to hire skis and have a few lessons. I'm really looking forward to it. I just have to provide spending money as the accommodation is free and Ruby has paid for my flight."

"She's very generous," Alistair remarks.

"Yes, I think it's because she knows how I missed out on the modelling contract. She says she can't walk down the aisle of a chemist that has

Mariel Cosmetics in it. Neither can I. It's just too upsetting."

"Do you think Ruby blamed her brother for you losing out on the modelling contract?" asks Jenny.

"Not especially, but I think she very much regretted involving her family."

*

They trot up the steps of a townhouse in a street overlooking Glasgow Botanic Gardens and ring the original Victorian doorbell. A bare-footed woman, with grey bobbed hair wearing fuchsia pink leggings and matching vest top, ushers them in out of the cold.

"Hello, hello. I'm afraid you've caught me in the middle of doing yoga."

Alistair replies, "I can assure you, Mrs Balding, we've caught people doing a lot worse."

They walk across a wide hall, decorated with oil paintings, mostly in elaborate gilt frames. "I'm trying out some new poses before I release them on my pupils. I'm just back from Norway where I was learning Forrest Yoga." She makes a gesture towards a sumptuous, mustard coloured, velvet sofa. "Please, take a seat. Would you like a glass of mineral water?"

"No thank you," replies Alistair.

"Green tea?"

"No, honestly we're fine."

"I'm sorry for your loss Mrs Balding."

"Losses" she corrects him. "In the last two years I have lost my husband and now my son."

"We need to ask you a few questions to clear some things up."

"Go ahead. I'll help in any way I can."

DI Gunn proceeds. "When was the last time you saw your son, Mrs Balding?"

Taking some time to consider the question, she replies, "I haven't seen my son, Inspector, since his father's funeral. Prior to that it was my birthday when we had dinner in the Rogano. That's when we told Simon and his sister that my husband, their father, had terminal cancer."

"How did his son take the news?"

"Better than expected. Or perhaps he was in denial. I don't know. Maybe he thought we were exaggerating the seriousness of it. Men are prone to burying their head in the sand, aren't they? Maybe he thought his father was making up an elaborate story to lure him back from London, I don't know."

"Was he supportive?"

"Who?"

"Your son."

"No, Inspector. That was the greatest shock for me. He was not supportive at all. He pretty much kept away, stayed in London, but he returned quickly enough to pick up the keys of the surgery which he inherited along with the brand new equipment his father had recently purchased."

"You were angry with your son?"

"Yes, I was angry and disappointed in him, but my yoga and meditation has helped hugely. 'Jesus said, forgive them for they know not what they do.' That is my philosophy now. I find it harder to forgive myself."

Lorna asks, "For what?"

The tears in Anne Balding's eyes turn on like a tap. She pulls a paper hanky from a box on a side table and dabs her eyes, "I'm sorry."

"Don't worry, take your time."

"Can you imagine what it's been like? Burying my son when I hadn't spoken to him in 18 months?"

"You weren't speaking to him when he died?"

Anne answers softly, "No, inspector, I wasn't. And I..." She pulls out another hanky then blows and rubs her nose "... have to live with that for the rest of my life."

To show respect, Lorna leaves a suitable pause before moving on. "I believe your daughter Ruby studied Philosophy?"

"Step-daughter. Yes, she did. She graduated in June." Her eyes fill with tears again. "If only her father could have been there."

"What about Ruby? How did she take the news when you told her? In Rogano I mean."

"Ruby asked all the questions under the sun, but when we explained there really was nothing more that could be done, that the cancer had spread, she literally broke down."

"Do you and Ruby have a good relationship?"

"Fairly good. Her biological mother died when she was just two years old. Ruby had a very special relationship with her father and sometimes I felt a little jealous, a bit left out, especially after our son left for university. That's why I took up meditation and believe me, it helps – hugely."

Alistair asks, "Do you have anything which belonged to your husband, Mrs Balding. "Something he might have touched?"

"Why do you ask that?"

"We're trying to establish whose finger prints are on the smoke alarm," explains Lorna.

"Why? What does it matter?"

"To establish if it was his finger print, or perhaps they belongs to the electrician who rewired the surgery? If the electrician knowingly left a smoke alarm up there, you could have a case of negligence."

"I can assure you, Inspector, I am not in the habit of suing people. I focus on positive energy now. Looking ahead to a brighter future. But if you really must examine my husband's finger prints, they'll be all over his workshop in the garden."

"Have you not cleared it?"

"No. He'd converted it into a darkroom. I left it just as it was in case anyone from the camera club wanted to use it, but they never have. It's full of his photographic prints – still hanging in a row from where he pegged them up. Examine anything you want if it helps you with your enquiry."

"Last question. Did you know there was a wasps' nest in the attic of the surgery?"

"My husband had talked about it, but he assured me a specialist company had destroyed it."

"So, he was no longer worried?"

"I've no idea, Inspector. My husband was good at keeping worries to himself. He was especially good at withholding the fact that he was ill."

*

The cellist glides her bow from side to side playing the bass notes of Ae Fond Kiss. The pianist, with the tail of his dinner suit draped over the back of the piano stool, tinkles the melody on the shiny, black grand piano.

Anne Balding closes her eyes to enjoy the last piece in what has been an enchanting concert of Scottish music in the entrance hall of Pollok house. She is seated next to her stepdaughter, Ruby. The pianist, Dr Nigel Wang, makes a beeline for them after he and his wife have bowed several times while soaking up the applause.

"Thank you for coming, Anne, Ruby."

Anne enthuses, "You were wonderful Nigel and so was Hannah. Ae Fond Kiss was my favourite. I just adored it."

"And you, Ruby, which one did you like best?"

"Possibly this one." Ruby points to 'Massacre of Glencoe' on the programme.

"I agree it's a lovely melody."

"Nigel," Anne explains, "we haven't just come tonight to enjoy the concert. We wanted to talk to you about the practice."

Nigel's face falls. "Are you planning to sell it?"

"No, not at all. Because my son didn't leave a will, Ruby and I will soon be joint owners so we'd like you to take over the running of it."

Nigel Wang raises his eyebrows.

Ruby adds, "On a much increased salary of course."

*

Using her keen, bright, brown eyes to scan passengers alighting from the train at Dundee railway station, Daisy spots her parents at the far end of the platform and walks briskly towards them. When she catches her dad's eye, she waves and runs the last stretch towards them. Her dad puts down his case and catches his daughter in his arms. A young black man with long dreadlocks and a brilliant white, generous smile approaches.

Daisy turns round to acknowledge him. "Mum, Dad, this is Freddie... from France."

Lorna says, "Hello, Freddie from France." They all shake hands.

Her dad urges, "Now, Daisy can you show us the way to this fancy hotel."

*

A bald man sits rigid on a hospital bed positioned in the middle of an empty room. He wears a hospital gown and sits cross-legged clutching a skull. His eyes are closed, his breathing slow. A gold gun, held in place by a wire hangs from the ceiling, points downwards towards his head. Low lighting amplifies the scene in shadow form on the walls behind him.

Lorna, Colin, Daisy and Freddie make up the bulk of the audience at this Cupar Arts Festival performance in the County buildings. The exhibit is titled, '*In my Bed, I'm My Guru*'. Daisy nudges her mum to leave as nothing has happened in the performance since they entered the room fifteen minutes earlier. The man, deep in meditation, hasn't moved an inch.

They cram into an independent coffee shop offering homemade baking and wait for Colin to return from the counter with four coffees, two pieces of carrot cake and four forks.

Freddie and Daisy are laughing. Freddie asks, "What was that about?"

Daisy replies, reading from the festival programme, "He is attempting to build an instant bridge between Life and Death... Well, that's what it says here."

Lorna is absorbed in her own thoughts. "Daisy, have you registered with a doctor yet?"

"Yes, Mum. Should I register with a dentist too?"

"I wouldn't bother."

"Why not?"

"It's this case I'm working on, Daisy. It's putting me off dentists. I mean, the money some of them earn is quite staggering. And how do we know when they're telling us the truth?"

"I have faith in my dentist in Lyon," replies Freddie. "And I have no fillings at all."

"I trust our dentist too, so you should continue to go to her, Daisy. You're not that far from home. Don't take any chances with a new one, okay?"

Colin arrives with the tray of goodies.

Daisy reassuringly touches Lorna's arm, "Stop fussing, Mum." Addressing Colin she says, "Dad, it makes sense to stop at the silo to see the light show on our way back to Dundee."

*

The electrician who rewired the dental surgery is tracked down to the Bridgeton area of Glasgow where he is renovating yet another tenement flat for his client who now owns hundreds. The owner is currently sunning himself in Barbados while Joe McIntyre's team carry out the hard graft.

Alistair parks the Volkswagen round the corner from the attractive red-roofed bandstand which reminds passers-by of the days when Bridgeton was a popular, thriving suburb. The clock tells the wrong time.

Jenny remarks, "The bandstand is nice."

"Ye mean the 'Brigton Umbrella'?"

They walk past bored-looking youths sitting on immovable concrete benches. The address of the flat they are looking for is situated in a three-storey tenement, sandstone building adjacent to the bandstand. Alistair presses the buzzer several times before a man shouts, accusingly, "Who is it?"

"It's the police. C.I.D. Come to see Joe McIntyre."

"You'd better come up," the voice replies politely.

They enter a room filled with stour. Two strong men are gathering up the remains of a demolished wall, the ceiling now propped up by a steel column.

Hard worker number 1 steps forward, "I'm Joe. Come into the kitchen – we can talk there."

Alistair asks, "Were you the contractor to refurbish 142 Glassford Street?"

"Mighta been."

"It's a dental surgery."

"The dentist Balding. Yeh, that wiz me. I mind thinking it was funny that he had a guid head o hair and wiz called Balding."

"Did you rewire his property?"

"Yes. I did all the work – plumbing, joinery, the lot."

"Did you install new smoke alarms?"

His face and voice pitch suggests irritation.

"Of course. I wired them up to the mains circuit. Why? are they no' working?"

"What did you do with the old ones?"

"I wid huv put them in the electrical section of the dump – and that's no cheap for a guy like me. Whit is this, anyway? What am I suppose to have done?"

"I have to ask these questions Mr McIntyre to establish whether Simon Balding's death could have been avoided."

"Did he no have cancer?"

"That was the father. The son, also called Simon Balding is dead too. He died last month from an anaphylactic reaction; killed by a swarm of wasps.

"What?"

"Simon Balding Junior disrupted a wasps' nest when he entered the attic trying to establish where a bleeping noise was coming from …"

"What are you on about?"

"…The beep, it turned out, was coming from an old smoke alarm, and judging by the layer of dust on it, had been there approximately twelve months."

Joe McIntyre crosses his hairy, thick, strong arms in defiance.

"You're accusing me of leaving an old smoke alarm in the attic, is that it?"

"We're not accusing you of anything, Mr McIntyre. We are just trying to establish how it got there."

Joe raises his voice, "Well, *I* didn't put it there. I wid never dae that. Never. I know how they things can be an awfy pest. I sacked an apprentice who chucked a pile of stuff in the basement of an auld woman's hoose. She became demented when she kept hearing bleeps fae underneath the floor boards. Her family thought she wiz going mad. She thought she was going mad. And it was all because of that untidy, lazy eejit."

"I'm not suggesting you left it there on purpose."

"I didn't leave it there full-stop. And I can prove it."

"How?"

"Because the finished work was inspected by a building control inspector, employed by the council."

*

Lorna pins up photos of possible suspects. They have been narrowed down to Simon Balding Senior deceased, Dr Nigel Wang, Simon Balding's mother and half-sister Ruby (the main beneficiaries of the will), Sophie Stewart and another customer who had tried, unsuccessfully to sue the victim; he has more or less been written off already as he is much too large to fit through the entrance to the attic.

Alistair tries to hide another delivery suspiciously shaped like it might be a golf club. He tries to deflect attention away from himself.

"How was Dundee, Boss?"

"Fantastic."

"I've only been there once to go to a football match. Looked a right dump."

"What???"

"…was a right climb up to Dens Park."

"You'd like it now, Alistair. The area is gearing up for The Open Championship coming next year to Carnoustie."

Lorna stands poised at her whiteboard.

"Now," she taps the board with a marker pen, "back to reality. What new information do you have for me? And it'd better be good. Alistair you go first."

"The electrician who rewired the surgery definitely didn't dump the smoke alarm in the attic."

"How can that be proved?"

"Since our visit to Bridgeton, I've spoken to the building inspector who was sent out to inspect Joe's work. He sent me a copy of the report. There was a section, giving marks to how well the electrician had cleared up at the end of the job. He had ticked off every room, including the attic and eaves and basement, noting they had been left in excellent order. The inspector's opinion is that Joe McIntyre is one of the best, most meticulous tradesmen in Glasgow."

"I'd better get his number."

"I don't know what more he can tell you, Boss."

Lorna smiles. "I'm thinking about when my own house needs rewiring. Whose next?"

"I tracked down the pest control company that had been called out to the surgery around the time of the renovation."

"Very good, Jamal. What's the name?"

"P.P.P. Pollok Pest Patrol." He turns and smiles smugly at Jenny.

She mouths the word "Sook" back at him forgetting she's twenty-six and not at school.

"Have you spoken to the company yet?"

"Yes, I called them."

"You didn't email?"

"No. Some people, especially tradesmen, ignore emails, not that I ever would."

"You'll be emailing acquaintances from your death bed, Jamal, if you don't watch out."

Alistair asks, impatiently, "So…what did the company say?"

"They said Simon Balding Senior called them out to deal with a wasps' nest in the attic. The nest was disturbed during the renovations."

"So if they were called out, why is the nest still active?" asks Lorna.

"The nest is still active because they couldn't reach it. They tried, but it was positioned in such a small space at the furthest point in the eaves that it was impossible to remove it. They were only able to spray the nest which is what they did."

"Didn't do a very good job then, did they? I think a refund's in order."

"The guy at Pollok Pest Patrol said problems with live wasps' nests often recur. He warned

Simon Balding Senior the problem might start up again next mating season." He flips open his notebook, "His exact words were, 'wasps are persistent little buggars'."

"Thanks, Jamal. Now…" Lorna waves her index finger over photographs pinned to her whiteboard. "…Who had keys to the surgery apart from our main suspect, Simon Balding Senior deceased? I don't see how Sophie Stewart could have had one."

"And she doesn't really have a proper motive," adds Alistair. "She may have flown off the handle at Simon Balding, but she admitted herself it wasn't bad dentistry that made her miss out on the modelling contract, it was unfortunate timing."

Lorna points to Anne Balding. "What about the mother? Does she have a motive?"

"She hadn't spoken to her son in nearly two years because," Alistair flips back a few pages in his notebook, "she said, 'Simon showed how narcissistic he was when his father lay dying."

"That doesn't prove anything."

"She's a very calm woman, Boss. Would never say anything out of turn. I could imagine her meticulously planning a murder."

Lorna points to Dr Nigel Wang. "What about this guy? He had a motive. Isn't he now in charge of the surgery?"

Jenny replies, "Only on a temporary basis, Boss. Jamal found a job advert online looking for a dentist to run the surgery. I contacted Anne Balding.

It seems Dr Wang turned down an offer of promotion to focus on his music. He made it very clear to her he never wants to be more than a salaried dentist. She was very disappointed."

"Okay, that rules him out. That just leaves Ruby Balding, his half-sister. Let's give her a visit."

*

At the entrance to one of Glasgow's best known auction houses, a queue forms at a van selling piping hot teas, coffees and rolls containing various greasy fillings. DI Gunn and Detective Sergeant Jenny Brown join the queue. They are surrounded by ordinary-looking people who have gone to great lengths to hide their wealth. Nothing, in the way the customers are dressed, gives away their intention to part with, in some cases, tens of thousands of pounds in exchange for art work. Today is a specialist auction for contemporary Scottish art incorporating painting, sculpture and photography.

"Jenny, if you could order a skinny latte for me that would be great."

"Is that all yer havin'? I'm going to get a square sausage roll for myself."

"In that case Jenny, could I have a bacon roll? No sauce. Bacon nice and crispy. I'll go inside and have a look around. See if I fancy bidding on anything."

"I had a look at the catalogue. The cheapest painting has an asking price of 800 pounds."

"Well, make sure you don't purchase anything by mistake, Jenny. Keep your hands firmly by your sides, don't nod and don't, whatever you do, tug at an itchy ear."

"2,760 pounds going once," The auctioneer scans the room. "Going twice," The auctioneer glances at a woman holding a mobile phone who has been taking telephone bids and at a man poised at a laptop passing on internet bids. The auctioneer hits his hammer against the lectern, "SOLD." He points at Ruby Balding. "To number 362."

"That's a lovely painting you have there, Miss Balding."

"And you are?"

Lorna produces her ID and adds softly, "Can we ask you a few questions, perhaps somewhere quieter?"

They move away from the throng of bidders who wait patiently for a painting or sculpture they have selected to be auctioned off. Anxious sellers, unaccustomed to the workings of auction houses, hope they will achieve more than the auctioneer has told them their ancestor's painting is worth.

Lorna is reminded of a time when, on the death of her mother, she invited an 'antique dealer' round to the house. The dealer had announced that everything was in fact worthless and made out he was doing her a great favour by clearing the house free of charge. She had later read he had been convicted at Greenock Sheriff Court for conning a woman into parting with an Oriental vase which he had immediately resold at an auction in New York for $95,000.

They sit down on brown leather art-deco armchairs intended for the furniture auction taking place tomorrow.

"So, how can I help you?" asks Ruby.

Jenny flips open her notepad.

Lorna asks, "Is it true you plan to open a gallery, Miss Balding?"

"It is."

"And you're only, what twenty...?"

"I'm thirty-two. Everyone thinks I'm younger." Jenny writes it down.

"And you're here to purchase paintings for the gallery. Is that right?" asks Lorna.

"Yes, but I'm also selling some Peter Howson pastels my dad bought from the Wasp studio thirty odd years ago. Before he was famous."

"Don't you like them?"

"They're brilliant, if a bit brutal." Ruby is careful to add, "In my opinion."

"Are they your paintings to sell?"

"When my father died, he left his small art collection to me and the surgery to Simon. The paintings were purchased when he was married to my mother, the real love of his life, but please don't tell Anne I said that. He was very fond of her, as am I."

Jenny asks, "Were you fond of your brother Simon?"

"Fairly, although he did upset Anne and me dreadfully after our father's diagnosis."

"In what way?"

"He only travelled up from London once to see him when he was dying. Simon's excuse was that he would lose his job if he neglected his rich clients in that fancy Harley Street practice he worked in. It's all about money down there, Inspector. They value little else."

Jenny realises she heard similar lines spoken recently by Dr Nigel Wang. "Did you fall out with your brother at this time, Miss Balding?"

"I couldn't speak to him at our father's funeral, I was too upset, but we have made up since. I organised a lovely marble gravestone for him next to our father's in Carmunnock Cemetery. He loved to play with marbles when he was little. His favourite game was Chinese Checkers. My grandparents left us a beautiful set with marble balls which was bought in Shanghai. Might be worth something now."

"Miss Balding, did you recommend your brother's dental practice to your friend following her cycling accident?"

Ruby thrusts her body back slightly in the chair. "What's Sophie got to do with this?"

"We have our reasons for asking. Did you recommend your friend Sophie Stewart go to your brother for dental work following a cycling accident?"

"I did... because he had about the best training a dentist could have - in Newcastle and London. I also thought he might give her a discount which he did."

The auction house begins to clear as art-loving customers leave carrying framed paintings and all manner of sculptures. Jenny closes her notebook. The two detectives stand up to leave.

"If there's anything else you need to know, or if you'd like to attend the private opening of my art gallery, please call me." Ruby produces a business card from her jacket pocket and hands it to Lorna. "The first exhibition is focusing on Scottish contemporary female artists."

"Thanks. Just one more thing." DI Gunn enjoys saying the famous line from the classic television detective series *Columbo*.

"Yes, Inspector?"

"Did your father discuss the problematic wasps' nest in the attic with you?"

"No, he didn't. I had no idea it was there. If I had, I would have warned Simon."

*

"**C**olin, I'm not sure you should be drinking whisky and listening to Eric Bogle songs when things are not going so well at work." The song, titled, *No use for him*, plays...

They took away his job
when they'd no use for him any more
After nearly thirty years
they kicked him out the door
But they let him keep his railway jacket,
overcoat, and cap
And a pension of nine bob a week,
he was lucky to get that.
But they nearly broke his heart,
when they'd no use for him.

"I left the drug squad to became a librarian to avoid stress." Colin takes a large sip from a crystal whisky glass.

"I know you did, Colin." She places a comforting hand on his shoulders. "But, why don't you play that record *All will be well* that Daisy gave you instead?... by the Dundonian...what's his name?"

"Michael Marra."

The song, *No use for him,* continues.

When you're fifty-five years old
and you're looking for some work
Nobody wants to know your face,

no-one gives you a start
So I watched him growing older
and more bitter every day…

Colin takes what is more like a gulp of whisky. "At least you know where you are with drug addicts. But these slimy politicians – they couldn't live on a librarian's salary and they think getting rid of us is going to reign in the country's deficit. Fat chance. I'm telling you Lorna, this country is finished. I wish a swarm of wasps would put me out of my misery."

As his pride and self-respect,
were slowly drained away
There was nothing I could say –
they had no use for him.

Lorna moves towards the record player and opens the lid.

"You don't mean that." She lifts the needle to stop the record and adds firmly, "Now, come to bed."

*

Lorna sits on a bench outside the beautiful, sandstone library building watching a variety of people, young and old come and go. A volunteer gardener is finishing off planting tulip bulbs in the flower beds in front of the library. He cheerily explains to Lorna his plan for them to be in bloom to coincide in Spring with a series of talks on Dutch literature.

A smiling child, wearing a duffle coat and wellingtons, carrying a large Paddington Bear picture book skips towards the entrance. She is holding the hand of an adult, possibly her father, who is holding several books under his other arm. The top one, she can make out, is a crime novel – the genre that Lorna and Colin, for obvious reasons, choose to avoid. The general public's fascination with crime has always amazed her.

It is Friday and the time is approaching five o'clock. Earlier today, the dedicated library staff were due to find out if their library is earmarked for closure. They have already been warned that thirty libraries in Glasgow have been deemed 'unviable'.

Colin and Lorna decided the previous evening that whether the outcome is good or bad they would have a 'pre-theatre' meal at their favourite restaurant in Bath Street. However, as soon as Lorna sees Colin's face as he exits the building, she can surmise there has been a good outcome for this particular library. He saunters over to greet her.

"Hello, Gorgeous." He kisses her and sits down.

"So, you're still in a job then?"

"For now. It's the smallest libraries that are being closed – all 156 of them throughout Scotland."

"Oh God!" she grimaces.

"400 libraries have already closed in England, Lorna."

"And the ones that are still open, they keep mucking about with. I mean, this converting study areas into cafés, what's that all about?"

"Study areas don't make money, Lorna. Can you believe they made the decision based on floor area of the building, not how deprived an area is or how socially isolated residents might be? They are such idiots."

They walk across the eerie space which was once the stadium of Third Lanark Athletic football club in the direction of Crosshill Railway Station. As they enter the station, they hear the sound of a train arriving at the platform below. They run down the stairs and manage, just in time, to hop on the train heading into the city centre.

Ten minutes later, the electronic doors open and they walk along the platform against a throng of commuters heading in the opposite direction. They queue in a line to purchase a ticket, before being able to escape through the barrier.

Lorna never tires of walking through this beautiful station where she used to meet Colin, when they were young, under the central clock. She looks up at the wooden exterior of the Central Hotel and imagines drinkers enjoying cocktails in the newly refurbished Champagne bar – with it's domed ceiling, marble columns and new, snazzy black and white flooring and long, mirrored bar.

She grabs Colin's arm. "Do you remember when the Central Hotel was a dump?"

"Ye mean before it became the 'Grand Central Hotel'."

"I thought the name was different."

"And we'd always end up there when we missed our train."

They exit Central Station on to Hope Street and pass a Big Issue Seller standing close to the bulky, bronze masked statue of a firefighter. Colin discreetly passes the man a fiver as he is deep in conversation with a customer.

"Is it a table for two?"

"Yes, please."

The waiter waves his arms around the empty restaurant. "Sit anywhere you like."

They settle at a table by the window and prepare to study the menu. Smartly dressed workers rush along the pavement directly outside, storming down the hill in the general direction of the station. Nosy passers-by glance inside.

"Colin, I was awake until 2 in the morning reading that book you gave me."

"Which one?"

"The Naked Civil Servant. Some of his one-liners are terrific – like, 'However low a man sinks he never reaches the level of the police."

They laugh heartily and only stops to order a bottle of the house red and the set menu.

Colin's voice quietens, "Lorna, you know how I'm a stickler for grammar?"

"Uh, huh." Lorna munches at a bread stick, waiting for her chicken liver pate starter to arrive.

"And that I have a fascination with cemeteries?"

"Uh, huh." She takes a sip of Italian chianti poured into her glass by the attentive waiter.

Colin waits for him to leave. "I went to the cemetery you told me the dentist who died from the wasp stings is buried in."

"Why?"

"I dunno. I like Carmunnock. Thought the fresh air would do me good."

"You're a strange man, Colin."

"Plenty of people are interested in cemeteries, Lorna. Anyway, it took me a while, but I found two gravestones with the name Simon Balding on them."

The starters arrive. "Thanks". She turns back to Colin and lowers her voice. "If they'd known the younger one would die so soon after his father, they might have secured a two for one offer from the funeral director."

"Poor humour, Lorna. Anyway, I noticed an out of place comma on the gravestone of the younger one."

"A comma?"

"Yes." Colin takes a little notebook from this trouser pocket. "I've written it down."

"Once a policeman always a policeman, eh?"

"The inscription said,

Simon Balding
(Apr 9, 1989 – Sept 23 2017)

*The song is ended, but
the melody lingers on.*

"A comma's okay there. Just a little old-fashioned, maybe."

"It's not that comma, Lorna. It's the next one.

Loving son of Anne and Simon, sister Ruby.

I mean, why the comma? Why not *Loving son of Anne and Simon and loving brother of Ruby*? or something like that? The comma makes the sentence cold. It states he has a sister called Ruby. Nothing more. And *The Song is ended, but the melody lingers on* can have a good or bad meaning.

"You mean, like the smell lingers on?"

"Exactly. My conclusion is that she hated him."

"You could well be right about that Colin, but it was she who organised the gravestone. After her husband's death, the mother hadn't spoken to her son at all."

PART THREE
CROWNING CONCLUSION

Jamal walks in waving a smoke alarm, visible inside a polythene sleeve. "The fingerprint analysis is in, Boss. Two people's prints are on it and the finger prints on the black and white photographs match one of them.

DI Gunn guesses, "Simon Balding Senior's?"

"Yip. His print is on the red test button."

"The other finger prints are only partial prints, they appear on both sides, but are too vague to find a definite match in our database, and of course only convicted criminals are on it. All that forensics could tell me is that they are 99% sure that it belongs to a small, adult male."

Alistair sighs, "That would rule out our two female suspects then."

"Not necessarily," Lorna reasons. "Both the mother and sister are calm enough and clever enough to know to wear gloves. They could have moved the alarm from any location and placed it in the attic without leaving finger or footprints by wearing plastic gloves and shoe coverings just as we do at any crime scene.

I do think knowing the identity of the other male would help though. We need to ascertain where the smoke alarm came from. Has it always been in the surgery or has it come out of another property, say his father's house?"

Jenny is still considering the news that the partial prints found on the smoke alarm belong to a small male. "What about Nigel Wang? He's not very tall, although his fingers are long and slender.

I noticed that when we interviewed him in his house. I thought they were perfect fingers for playing the piano."

"No, the finger print on the light switch doesn't match the prints on the side of the smoke alarm. They're not his. I really think it's time we searched the homes of Anne and Ruby Balding. Look for any signs that a smoke alarm has been removed. Any freshly painted ceilings. Look for any make or model which doesn't match the rest."

*

A young man throws open the solid, wooden door. He is wearing glasses, red underpants and white socks.

Two uniformed police officers shows their IDs and search warrant. "We have a warrant to search this property."

His youthful eyes become shifty as he tries to think where he left the joint of weed he has been saving for the weekend. "My girlfriend's not in."

"Is your girlfriend Ruby Balding?"

"Might be."

"Don't be smart, son. Is she?"

"Yes."

"Where is Ruby?"

"Out running."

Just then Ruby comes bounding up the stairs, panting. On seeing the uniformed policemen she pulls out her earphones.

"Are you Ruby Balding?"

"Yes." She leans against the wall trying to recover.

"We have a warrant to search your flat." They hand her a printed sheet. The address at the top is hers.

The boyfriend butts in, "D'you not need to tell us what you're searching for?"

"It's all written in the warrant, son. We have reason to believe the alarm found in the attic of Simon Balding's surgery may have come out of this flat. We need to search the premises. Can we come in?"

Ruby gestures towards the door. "On you go." The officers push past her puny boyfriend.

Meanwhile a similar search is taking place a fifteen-minute walk away in Simon Balding's mother's home. When the police arrived at her door, Anne asked if it would be okay to continue her meditation practice in the peace room. The reply had been, "That's fine. We'll search the rest of the house first so as not to disturb you."

Anne sits cross-legged, meditating and chanting at intervals while officers examine smoke alarms and interior decoration throughout the rest of her home. A candle gives off a pleasant, jasmine aroma. She picks up a wooden mallet and brushes it gently around the perimeter of a Tibetan singing bowl, then closes her eyes and focuses on each chakra in her body. To finish her practice, she chants over and over the Hindu mantra 'om namah shivaya'. Eventually the police officers enter her inner sanctum. She opens her eyes.

"Well, have you found what you are looking for?"

"I can't really say, Ma'am." The officer glances round the room at her Hindu artefacts. "Have you found what you're looking for?"

"Oh, I think so," she replies, smiling to reveal a beautiful set of pristine, white teeth.

*

As the door to his office opens, Alistair quickly shoves a book under a pile of papers on his desk. Lorna senses he's hiding a golf book.

"What's that you're reading, Alistair?"

"Nothing."

She places a mug of tea for him on his desk then moves the papers to reveal a book titled *Indoor Golf Practice*.

"Caught. Red-handed." Lorna laughs heartily. "So, how did you like Machrihanish then? Did you end up on the beach?"

"That's two questions. Yes it was fantastic." He smiles smugly, "and no I didn't land on the beach. I was in plenty of rough though."

Lorna, a mug in her hand, walks over to the window as a police car screeches into the car park. The officer in the passenger seat jumps out, opens the back door and pulls out a youth. They escort him, handcuffed, towards the main entrance as he shouts obscenities at them. The young man is wearing an orange tracksuit. "Did you know Mandarin's back from Majorca?" She spots a putter jammed behind a filing cabinet.

"The Lodge'll be pleased. About this case, Boss. There's something I'm still not getting."

"What's that?"

"If the smoke alarm came out of Ruby's home why would it have her father's finger print on it?"

"Because, Alistair, it was Simon Balding who bought the flat for his daughter to live in while she was at university, so she could rent out rooms to other students and turn a profit. That explains why Ruby wasn't living at home. She was also a mature student." She takes a sip of piping hot tea. "It was he who put up a smoke alarm in every room to satisfy fire regulations. The lab has analysed the finger prints on all the alarms taken from Ruby's flat and they all bear his print on the test button. The lounge was the room most recently decorated – by a painter called Billy Samson from Denistoun. Forensics are 90% sure the partial finger print on the smoke alarm found in the dentist's attic matches his.'

"So this proves what exactly?"

"This proves, Alistair, that the smoke alarm came out of Ruby's flat. Billy's prints are on the edges because he took it down. The alarm was taken from the living room. It is the only alarm with two sets of finger prints. This proves the decorator touched only that one. And, apart from the bathroom, the living room is the only room without a smoke alarm on the ceiling."

"I think it'll take a while for Mandarin to get up to speed on this case."

"Every case more like," replies Lorna.

"We still don't know how the alarm ended up in the eaves of the attic though, do we?"

"Someone with a key to the surgery put it there."

"Mandarin'll go berserk when he discovers we're still working on this case."

Lorna walks towards the door and adds under her breath, "Yeh, he doesn't care who we nail for a crime as long as the arrest is quick and they're Catholic."

"Hey, I heard that," replies Alistair, former head boy of St Mungo's High School, "And you're probably right about that, Boss."

*

Radio 1 blares from a ghetto blaster in contrast to the elegant drawing room being decorated in a townhouse in Park Terrace by master painter Billy Samson. Lorna and Alistair stand on the doorstep while Alistair rings the doorbell incessantly and bangs on the enormous door.

Looking through sections of glass in the door, Lorna admires the opulent hall with marble flooring and Roman columns. She mutters, "Oh, how the other half live."

Leaning over the railing, Alistair sees the painter in action through the living room window. Billy is balancing himself on the top of a ladder in order to reach the cornicing. It's obvious he cannot hear them for the dreadful, loud music.

"I'd better not bash on the window in case he falls off the ladder."

Billy Samson is engrossed, pressing his soft brush into the intricate egg and bead cornicing. Alistair places his hand flat above his eyes to peer more clearly through the glass.

"I reckon my home could fit in to this one room."

"Alistair, this could take a while. Fancy running down to the van at Charing Cross and buying us something to eat?"

"Yeh, okay I'm starvin'."

"I'll wait here."

"That's good of you."

"Sarcasm, Alistair, is the lowest form of wit."

He sprints off in the direction of Woodland's Road while Lorna sits on the steps enjoying the view over Kelvingrove Park and the city beyond. Her eyes scan from left to right picking out the most recognisable landmarks like the Armadillo and Glasgow University Tower.

To kill time, she walks round to Park Circus to see the former registry office where she, Colin and half of Glasgow were married. An Italian social club and consulate before that, it was possibly the grandest venue for civil marriages in Britain. Lorna thinks of the photograph she has at home, in a silver frame, of them kissing up on the 1st floor gallery under the arch, showing some of the ornate glazed dome. That was the photographer's idea. She wonders how many couples have a similar photo on their mantelpiece.

She reaches number 22. The door is now closed, the steps empty, devoid of confetti, and the street deserted. She had heard on the news that the council's lease finally ran out and, when the building was sold, it signalled the end of an era. If she and Colin had been able to afford the asking price of £1.5 million, they may well have bought it.

When she returns, Alistair is sitting half-way up the steps of the Park Terrace property with a collection of small paper bags. He hands her one. "That one's for you. It has no sauce on it."

Lorna sits down beside him. "Thanks Alistair." She examines the roll. "You got me a potato scone too. Nice."

"Don't say I'm not good to you."

"I would never say that." She bites into the delicious roll and munches. "Much better than the ones we get back at the station."

"You're not kiddin'."

"We should have stayed at Pitt Street, Alistair."

He laughs, "That old chestnut."

Suddenly, the music stops, they hear steps frantically running down the hall, then panting. The door opens and a Springer Spaniel rushes out, pushing past them as it bounds down the stairs.

The man following the dog out, stops to lock the door, then shouts, "Delilah!" When he sees them sitting on the steps he apologises. "Sorry about that. She's been cooped up all morning, the poor thing."

Lorna and Alistair stand up, hastily brush crumbs from their clothes, and show their IDs to a man clearly no more than five-foot-two-inches tall.

Alistair says, "We're investigating events around the death of the dentist Simon Balding."

Billy screws up his face. "He died of cancer. I'm no a scientist."

"I'm referring to the death of Simon Balding Junior. He was only 28."

"His son. Oh, that's tragic." Billy adds, "I didn't know him though."

The sun reveals itself from behind a cloud and projects warm golden light onto Glasgow's famous park. It is turning into a beautiful winter's day.

"Do you mind if we walk with you, Mr Samson?"

"Come if you want. How d'you know where I wiz working the day?"

Alistair responds, "Your Facebook page."

Billy Samson glares at him.

"I'd watch that if I were you," warns Alistair. "Boasting, I mean 'posting' information on social media for everyone to see lets burglars know where you are."

"I didnae think a that."

They pass through an entrance into Kelvingrove Park.

"Mr Samson, how long have you been carrying out work for the Balding family?"

"I dunno. Maybe five year."

"Are you friendly with the family?"

"Naw, I'm just the dogsbody."

Delilah, flopping her ears like mad from side to side runs into a flowerbed crushing the flowers. She squats under a pink Camellia bush which has been neatly clipped into a perfect tree shape by a park department gardener.

"D'you have a bag on your person, Mr Samson?" asks Alistair, irritated.

"Yes. Would you arrest me if I didn't."

"It is an offence, Mr Samson under the THE DOG FOULING (SCOTLAND) ACT 2003."

"Is that no only if yer dug fouls on a footpath or pavement?" He takes a little spade from his pocket and digs a small hole to bury his dog's mess.

Lorna raises her voice slightly, "Mr Samson, what was the last job you did for the Balding family?"

"I painted a room in the daughter's flat...in" Billy gazes upwards while rubbing his chin. "Lawrence Street – it's a braw flat at the far end away fae Byres Road. Nice and quiet." Lorna imagines the peace and quiet would be shattered once Billy got to work.

"Did you carry out any work in Simon Balding's dental surgery?"

"Yeh. Painted the whole place inside and out. He'd just had it done up. Rewired and everything."

Alistair responds, "There's no record of that."

Billy Samson looks sheepish, "Ah, well…"

"Was it a cash in hand job?"

"Look," He raises his hands in the air, "I'm one of the good guys. I don't sign on. I put *almost* everything through the books. Look, it was the dentist who suggested it, nae me."

"Billy, can you explain why your finger prints are on an old smoke alarm found in the eaves of Simon Balding's dental surgery?"

After a few moments silence, Billy replies, "They can't be. On that job I didn't remove *one* smoke alarm because they were all running off mains electricity. I leave that type well alane and paint round them."

"Did you take a battery powered smoke alarm down from the ceiling when you painted Ruby Balding's living room?"

"Youse are trying to frame me. I didnae do nothing."

"You've done time for assault Billy, isn't that why you spent two years in the Bar-L?" Alistair reminds him.

"I've no' been in trouble with the polis for ten year. Can you no leave me alane?"

Lorna answers, "That is admirable, Billy, but can you please answer the question? Did you take a smoke alarm down from the ceiling when you painted Ruby Balding's living room?"

Billy is flustered. "I cannae mind. If there was one stuck tae the ceiling I would huv taken it doon to paint it. Saves time in the long run cause I can use the roller uninterrupted."

"What do you normally do with items you remove from walls and ceilings, Billy?"

"I didnae nick them if that's what you're getting at. I leave everything I tak' doon the gether so nothin' gets lost – pictures, picture hooks, mirrors, clocks, that type of thing. It would tak' ower lang tae pit everything back up. I leave that tae the customers. I work hard enough."

Billy Samson puts two fingers in his mouth and whistles. "Come on Delilah. Time to go." Delilah runs further into the park.

*

Lorna points at a photograph of the painter and decorator. "I don't see that Billy even has a motive. But, most crucially, he decorated the surgery before he decorated Ruby's flat. For him to be in the frame, he would have had to decorate the surgery after the flat. In fact it was the other way round. Yes, he took the smoke alarm down from the ceiling, but he couldn't have placed it in the eaves of the surgery unless he had stolen a key and copied it."

Alistair points at a photograph of Ruby Balding. "Whereas the sister has an almighty motive. Once Simon married, in the event of his death, his sister would have no claim to the business or his luxury penthouse apartment on Clyde Street unless his will stated otherwise. Everything, would automatically go to his spouse."

"Of course, the other chief suspect remains Simon Balding Senior. He died in a hospice here in Glasgow. Let's go there and find out if he said anything significant about his son to the staff while he lay dying. Did he hate him enough to set the trap?"

*

Lorna and Alistair marvel at the optimistic atmosphere and the stunning views of the courtyard garden as they pass by floor-to-ceiling windows inside the hospice building.

A middle-aged woman with the warmest smile shows them to an empty sitting area. "Chris is with a patient right now, but shouldn't be long."

"This place. It's not what I was expecting."

"I knew it'd be nice," replies Lorna. "These Maggie centres are famous for their uplifting architecture."

A young man walks across the room heading in their direction.

Alistair whispers, "Don't know why I was expecting a woman."

"With a name like Chris?"

"My Aunt Christine calls herself Chris."

They stand up as the male nurse introduces himself then settle back down into the comfy chairs. Alistair takes his notebook from his pocket to indicate an end to their informal conversation.

Lorna asks, "Do you remember a patient called Simon Balding?"

"I nurse a lot of patients, Inspector Gunn."

She produces a photo from her briefcase. "He was a dentist."

"Oh yeh. I nursed him. He was a lovely man. Had prostate cancer."

"Can you remember any details about him? Like who visited him regularly?"

"His wife and daughter visited, I think, every day he was in here. But rarely together."

"You think they didn't get on?"

"No, I don't think it was that. A lot of relatives visit separately just so the patient receives more visits. Also, at the end of someone's life, the conversation can become very personal and tiring so we usually recommend only one person enter the room at a time."

Lorna produces a photograph of Simon Balding Junior.

"Do you know if this man visited?"

"I don't recognize the face, but he might have. You'd have to ask Matron to look at our records. Everyone signs in and out."

Lorna shows photographs of Anne Balding and Ruby which he recognises and names correctly.

"Do you remember any unusual details about Simon Balding's end of life experience?"

Chris looks away, pauses then adds, "I remember the last thing he said."

"Do you?" Lorna is taken aback.

"I remember it because at the time I thought it was a bit odd."

"Was anyone else in the room at the time?"

"Ruby was alone in the room, sitting in a bedside chair. I was listening at the door. I was waiting for an appropriate time to enter to check his breathing, as we have to do at certain intervals. "

Alistair is impatient. "And what did you hear Simon Balding say?"

"I heard Simon Balding say, and he said it gently, with his last breath, "Please tell Simon about the wasps' nest."

*

Ruby gracefully glides from side to side, as if it's the most natural thing in the world to descend on skis from the highest peak in Verbier. Arriving at the bottom, she skis across country to the nursery slopes where Sophie has been receiving lessons. Ruby spots her lying on her back in the snow, laughing. Sophie is helped up by Ruby's friend and ski instructor Toby, who spends his summers caddying at St Andrews in Scotland, and his winters teaching skiing in Verbier. He seems never to want to grow up.

Ruby calls out, "Don't worry, Sophie. You'll soon get the hang of it."

"You reckon?" Sophie removes tinted ski goggles from her eyes and places them on top of her helmet.

"A bit more practice and you'll soon be one of us. Come on, the others are waiting for us back at the chalet. They're chomping at the bit to hit the bars."

They trudge back to the roadside and Ruby helps Sophie to unclip her skis. They walk back along the road, through the picturesque village, and make the short climb, carrying their skis over their shoulders, to the chalet while Ruby boasts about the après-ski in Verbier and the great times she had spent there as a child.

*

When their plane touches down in Glasgow the following evening, Ruby and Sophie laugh and joke as they saunter down the gangway together.

"Back to reality," Ruby says stepping onto familiar Scottish soil.

The two young women follow the herd through passport control and, while they wait for their enormous suitcases to be delivered, Sophie calls her dad to let him know they've landed. Finally, pushing a laden trolley, the last set of automatic doors slide open. As other travellers eyes light up with joy when they catch sight of their loved ones, Ruby's turn to terror when she realizes DI Lorna Gunn and Alistair Boyle have come to greet *her*.

Ruby, trying her best to sound casual, asks, "What are you doing here?"

Alistair takes out a piece of paper and reads, "Ruby Balding, I'm arresting you on suspicion of murdering your half-brother Simon Balding."

"What? You're off your heads," Sophie protests. "Simon was killed by wasps. It was an accident. Everyone knows that. Tell them, Ruby."

Ruby, her face now the colour of snow, turns to face Lorna. Alistair continues, "There is no obligation for you to say anything until a solicitor is present."

Ruby responds by saying nothing at all.

D I Gunn and DC Boyle sit at a table in the police interview room facing Ruby Balding and her lawyer. DI Gunn presses a button on a recording device.

DI Gunn: This interview is being recorded. The date is 18 December 2017, the time is 10:30 a.m. by my watch. I am DI Gunn and I am based at Glasgow police headquarters, Dalmarnock. I work in the Serious Crime Squad. What is your name?'

Ruby: Ruby Balding.

DI Gunn: Can you confirm your date of birth for me?

Ruby: 8 March 1985.

DI Gunn: Thank you. Also present is...

DC Boyle: DC Boyle.

DI Gunn: Also present is Ruby Balding's lawyer...

Lawyer: Robert Neilson.

DI Gunn: What is your current occupation, Ruby?

Ruby: Gallery owner.

DI Gunn: What is your address?

Ruby: Flat 1/1, 126 Lawrence Street, Glasgow.

DI Gunn: What is your relationship with Simon Balding?

Ruby: He is, I mean was, my half-brother.

DI Gunn: Did you know he was allergic to wasps?

Ruby: I do remember him not being very well when he was stung as a child, but I didn't know a wasp sting could be fatal.

DI Gunn: His medical records state that when he was fourteen he was hospitalized for two weeks and very nearly died.

Ruby: I had no idea the situation was that serious. I was not aware of it.

DI Gunn: Why did you not inform your brother about the wasps' nest in the attic?

Ruby: I didn't know of the nest's existence.

DI Gunn: Well, we know that isn't true, Miss Balding. We have a witness who overhead your father's last words. They were, "Please tell Simon about the wasps' nest."

Ruby: I was alone in the room with my father at the end.

DI Gunn: A nurse was listening at the door, Miss Balding. Waiting to enter. So why didn't you tell him? Why?

Ruby: I forgot. With the funeral and everything…

DI Gunn: You forgot to tell him something that could have saved his life. And he was your brother.

Ruby: The wasps might not have returned. He might never have looked in the attic.

DI Gunn: Is that why you planted a smoke alarm up there, with an even older battery in it, to ensure he did?

Ruby:	No.
DI Gunn:	We know the smoke alarm came out of your flat.
Ruby:	Rubbish.
DI Gunn:	It had your painter and decorator's finger prints on it.
Ruby:	I'm sure Billy Samson decorates a lot of houses, Inspector.
DI Gunn:	But not all houses will have smoke alarms with your father's finger prints on them too.
Ruby:	The alarm could have come out of my dad's house or been in the surgery all along. I don't know.
DI Gunn:	Who do you think might have put the smoke alarm in the attic?
Ruby:	The electrician?
DI Gunn:	The electrician removed the old smoke alarms, not Billy Samson. We can also prove he left nothing behind after he rewired the surgery.
Ruby:	Dad then?
DI Gunn:	He was lying in a hospice when your living room was being decorated, Miss Balding. We are in no doubt that the smoke alarm came out of your flat. As well as the finger printing evidence on it, it matches the make and model to the others still present in your home.
Ruby:	You're confusing me.

DI Gunn: And we know you knew about the wasps' nest. So why don't you start by telling me the truth, Miss Balding? Why didn't you inform your brother about the wasps' nest?

Ruby: …Because I was angry with him. He let down my father who had ferried him here there and everywhere when he was a child. A very spoilt child.

DI Gunn: Were you jealous of him?

Ruby: Not really. He had also inflicted harm on my friend. I just wanted him to suffer a bit for what he had done.

DI Gunn: Please tell me Ruby. What had your brother done?

Ruby: He caused and still causes anguish to my friend Sophie who is in a lot of debt.

Di Gunn: We know about the cycling accident and we also know Sophie Stewart's teeth couldn't be saved. It wasn't Simon's fault she lost the modelling contract.

Ruby: Well, that's just it, Inspector, *that* I know is categorically untrue.

DI Gunn: Let's have your version of events then?

Ruby: By chance I met the dentist who treated her at the time of the accident. The guy who took the temporary brace off. He remembered me well because at the time I had blue hair. I was hard to forget.

DI Gunn: When and where did you meet him?

Ruby: In a bar, shortly after she'd had the implants fitted. He was adamant Sophie did not need to have her front teeth pulled out. He said he doubted after a few months she'd even have required root canal treatment. He said the worst case scenario was she might possibly have needed an extraction in several years time, but only after root canal treatment had failed.

DI Gunn: The consultant told you all this...?

Ruby: He was a bit drunk at the time.

DI Gunn: But I thought?

Ruby: My brother was a liar, Inspector. The only reason he pulled Sophie Stewart's front teeth out was to make money. And that, Inspector, is the sad truth. Simon didn't even try root canal treatment. He didn't even offer it. He went straight in for the kill and he knew she was not from a well-off family, and that she made money from her looks. How sick is that, Inspector? And I recommended him. My own brother did that to me.

DI Gunn: Did you tell Sophie?

Ruby: I didn't have the heart to. What good would it have done? It wouldn't have brought back the modelling contract or stopped the bank or loan sharks hounding her for money.

DI Gunn: And the dental hospital consultant, he was absolutely certain was he – that Sophie's teeth didn't need taken out at all?

Ruby: Absolutely certain. When I told him that Simon had whipped Sophie's teeth out with a pair of pliers and that she had got into horrendous debt in order to receive his brutality, he was horrified. As was I. I'm not like Anne. I couldn't let him get away with it. But I didn't mean any serious harm to come to him, Inspector. I didn't imagine for a minute the wasps stings could be fatal.

DI Gunn: I think we'll finish there Miss Balding. This interview is now terminated. The time is 11:00.

Chief Inspector Darren Russell has summoned Lorna to his office because he needs her to solve one remaining clue to complete the complex puzzle.

Lorna sits down opposite her superior. "What's the clue?"

Her suntanned superior picks up a folded *Herald* newspaper and replies, "Boy and girl may experience this after probe by small creature. Eleven letters and the last one is an s."

Lorna hesitates, then has a light-bulb moment. "I think I know it, sir."

"Well, Lorna," Darren Russell urges, "what is it?"

She smiles smugly and replies, "It's *anaphylaxis*, sir."

"How d'you spell it?"

"A n a p h y l a x i s."

"It fits. Oh well done, Lorna. I knew you'd figure it out." He puts down the paper. "Now about this wasp case, Lorna. Do you really think any jury could find this lassie guilty of murder?"

"Possibly not, sir, but she is, one way or another, responsible for her brother's death."

"Families eh?"

"Ruby Balding has a good lawyer, so most likely the charge will be reduced to one of culpable homicide."

"Considering what that rogue dentist did to that bonny lassie, the judge might be lenient."

"That's what I'm hoping, Sir."

Chief Inspector Darren Russell pulls out a pair of scissors from a drawer and cuts out the completed cryptic crossword ready for posting.

If you've enjoyed reading *Dental String* the author would be most grateful if you would leave a positive review on either Amazon or Goodreads. Any constructive criticism is appreciated.

Book 1 in the Inspector Gunn series is *Concrete Alibi*.

Cover image: The Glasgow School of Art

Concrete Alibi is a murder mystery set in Glasgow featuring a professor of architecture who is so conceited he may even deserve to be bumped off. Detective Inspector Lorna Gunn sets out to discover who loathed him enough to do it.

Includes no bad language or gratuitous violence.

Book 3 in the Inspector Gunn series is *Criminal Lawyer*.

Cover image: High Court of Justiciary in Glasgow

Detective Inspector Lorna Gunn investigates the sudden death of a recently retired criminal defence lawyer found slumped over a card table, having played his last ever game of Solitaire.

Includes a bit of humour, no bad language or gratuitous violence.

Printed in Great Britain
by Amazon